The Hunt

Katie Hall

Order this book online at www.trafford.com
or email orders@trafford.com

Most Trafford titles are also available at major online book retailers.

Printed in Victoria, BC, Canada.

ISBN: 978-1-4269-2935-9 (sc)
ISBN: 978-1-4269-2936-6 (eb)

*Our mission is to efficiently provide the world's finest, most comprehensive
book publishing service, enabling every author to experience success.
To find out how to publish your book, your way, and have it available
worldwide, visit us online at www.trafford.com*

Trafford rev. 05/13/2010

www.trafford.com

North America & international
toll-free: 1 888 232 4444 (USA & Canada)
phone: 250 383 6864 ♦ fax: 812 355 4082

For Kenny;

Honestly, without you none of this could be possible.
You're an inspiration and I love you more than
words can articulate.
Thank you so much Doll Face.

For my Dad;

I wish you were here to see this.
You would have been so proud.
I miss you everyday. I love you, R.I.P.

And for Mom;

You're so supportive and loving.
Thanks for always believing in me.
I love you, always.

Acknowledgments

Thanks to Shantel and Jenny, without whom I wouldn't have had the courage to go through with any of this. Thanks for being my editors and my friends, you two are amazing.

And, thanks, to Emma Reid. I would never have chosen this as a career if it hadn't been for you. Thank you from the bottom of my heart for pointing me in the right direction. I probably would have been a Vet if it weren't for you.

And to everyone else, I love you all dearly.

One

Snow fell gently from the black sky, covering my long auburn hair with a white veil of perfect snowy stars. I tightened my scarf as I looked up. This time of year was my personal favourite; it was beautiful and magical. It was hard to explain really, but I loved everything about it, the snow most especially.

I looked down in time to hit my face off of someone's shoulder. I almost fell backwards, muttering an apology just as strong hands wrapped around my wrists and pulled me back to my feet. I looked up and was almost rendered speechless by the deep intensity of the emerald eyes that met my own honey coloured ones.

"Are you okay?" The voice was deep and husky with the accent it carried; Irish maybe? I couldn't be sure.

I smiled and hoped to God it didn't look like the hopeless kind. "Yeah," I replied, moving out of his grasp as I tried to examine his face. "Are you?"

He smiled and it literally took my breath away. He had those perfect sensual lips that made you want to kiss them until you forgot your own name. He had jet black hair, curled slightly at the ends where it flopped onto his forehead. His face was beautiful, the kind of face you'd expect to see on an avenging angel. There was no doubt about it, he was a gorgeous man, and I was staring at him like a fool, how original.

"I'm smashing." he replied, running his gaze over me the way I had just done to him. "You're sure you're okay, love?"

I shot him what I hoped was a dazzling smile and nodded, "Thanks for keeping me upright." I laughed slightly, stuffing my hands into my long coat. "Have a good night."

He frowned at me and it looked so perfect on his incredible face that I wanted to applaud. "Where are you headed?" A startlingly mischievous smile toyed with his lips and I hated that it made my stomach do a somersault.

"Just to the Grocery store, I need to stock up on things Genevieve doesn't carry." I frowned, wondering why I was sharing so much with a stranger I'd bumped into on a cold city street.

His grin was amazingly feral; a glint of something I couldn't catch in time glimmered in the depths of his perfect green irises. "I was just headed to the store myself. Mind if I join you?"

I didn't, but I didn't want him to know that. "If you were going to the store why were you headed in the wrong direction?"

He winked at me; a cocky smile twisting his perfect grin. "Maybe I wanted to run into such a pretty lady."

I smiled tightly, looking up at least a foot and a half to meet his eyes. "I'm flattered, really, but I don't have time for this. Thanks for saving me from hurting myself." I moved away, heading for the light that bathed the corner of the street where I knew the store would be.

But he wasn't the type to give up so easily. He caught up with me in two long strides and matched my pace evenly, watching me as we walked. "Genevieve is a really small town." he said it conversationally, a smile in his voice.

"Yep, it's got a population of a hundred and fifty people."

"That's a lot smaller than Vase Line."

I felt my eyes narrow but I didn't turn to him. We were in Vase Line, the only real city for miles and separated from Genevieve by a thick smattering of forestry. It had nearly quadruple the amount of people than Genevieve did and a hell of a lot more stores.

"What's your name?"

I stopped and turned to him, my gaze flitting from his cocky grin to his snow covered black hair to his exquisite emerald eyes. "I don't live here and I don't plan to stay long. I didn't mean to bump into you and I apologized, what more could you possibly want from me?"

He smiled, his eyes glittering with pleasure, "Just a name, love."

I frowned as I looked at him, noticing for the first time a peculiar hue in his eyes. I moved forward, meeting his gaze even as his eyes widened in surprise and then narrowed with something else entirely.

When I was within inches of him I looked up again. "Compulsion doesn't work on me." I whispered with a smile.

His grin never faltered. "Don't know what you're talking about, love"

I nodded, stepping away, "Sure you don't. Goodbye."

"What, not even a name?"

I walked backwards, flashing him my best smile. "The name's Gray." I said, offering him a delicate but hopefully seductive wink. "It's been lovely."

He tipped an invisible hat in my direction before winking out, leaving the street dark and sadly empty of his alluring and sunny presence. I wondered briefly if I would ever see him again and then hoped I wouldn't. I could handle being an outcast in Genevieve and I could even handle coming into Vase Line once a week to buy my Grams groceries but I couldn't handle a man like that no matter how much I wanted to.

I sighed as I turned around and moved into the grocery store, my smile wide and my body thrumming with adrenaline.

Grams wouldn't be happy about this.

Two

"Was he atleast discreet?" Grams asked about half an hour later back in Genevieve. She was putting the groceries away while I sat by the fireplace in the kitchen, a hot cup of coffee in my hands.

"Not in the least." I replied, working hard to keep my expression blank. "But no one was out and no one saw us."

Grams was a thin woman of about sixty with waist length white hair and intense golden eyes. She was beautiful with a face that hinted at a drop-dead-gorgeous past. She was graceful and poised, both of which I completely lacked. "How could you possibly know that?"

I rolled my eyes when she turned her back. "I can't for sure but no one was on the street."

Grams grumbled something unintelligible and then said loudly. "*Anyone* could have been watching Grace."

"I know that Grams."

We glared at each other; golden eyes against honey toned ones. But I offered her a smile as a white flag and the heat in her eyes died down, slightly. "If you want you could always go into Vase Line on Friday instead of sending me. No one would ever try to hit on you Grams, not the way you glare at people."

Her eyes narrowed but she didn't respond. She wouldn't go into Vase Line for a reason she'd never told me. But, like in Genevieve, our kind were not welcome with open arms, which was why we were careful to be discreet and stay out of the watchful eye of law enforcement and busybody neighbors who would more than likely report us to government agencies that would cage and dissect us on the grounds of scientific research.

Grams was afraid of that I think most of all. She would never be caged, she'd rather die than ever have her will and freedom stripped away like that, and I didn't blame her. But Grams, like all the other women in my family, was too proud to admit when she was afraid.

Grams and I tried to live our lives as mortal as possible while staying true to our Wiccan heritage in secret. Like other witches I grew up knowing what I was and then, when I was fourteen, I was initiated in the name of the elements and the Goddess, as a full-fledged witch. Some witches were allotted one power along with the ability to perform, cast and create spells and potions while others were just like the mortals, though they practiced and celebrated the Wiccan traditions.

Sadly, however, I haven't gotten my power yet, even after I was initiated. This worried me but also relieved me, if I didn't have anything to show I could pretty much live my life normally without the fear of accidentally using my magick on some unsuspecting human.

"Gray, are you listening to me?" Grams interrupted, now sitting across from me in her chair.

I shook my head, sipping my coffee before I met her eyes. "What were you saying?"

Grams frowned and I could almost see her thoughts flit across her face. "What's wrong with you?"

"Nothing," I said, swallowing the last of my cold coffee with a grimace. "What did you say?"

"Nothing, never mind," She frowned, her brows furrowing and I fought the urge to glare.

Instead I yawned loudly and smiled at her. "I'm going to bed." I said, "'Night Grams."

"Goodnight Gray."

I fled without another word. I didn't know why she was so worried about a guy we more than likely would never see again, or why she was so reluctant to go to Vase Line herself. But it didn't matter now, she wouldn't tell me and there was nothing I could do about it.

I closed my door and moved to turn on my stereo, letting the heavy instrumental fill the room as I paced, trying to figure things out. The main thing on my mind was the startlingly gorgeous man I'd met in Vase Line and the fact that he seemed so carefree. One thing I'd always wanted to feel and never had the chance to.

The second thing was how odd Grams was being. I knew she wanted us to be careful but the burning times were long gone, two hundred and thirty years gone to be exact. So why was she still so afraid of the humans?

I didn't have any answers to that and knew I wouldn't get any. Grams was a stubborn old broad and I've never been able to get anything out of her that she wasn't willing to divulge. She wouldn't tell me her problem with the humans or her problem with Vase Line, of that I was positive.

My gaze fell on a picture of my mom, taken the year before she died. She was beautiful, at twenty; her hair was the same colour as mine and her eyes a shade between mine and Grams'. But her smile was bright and glowing as she looked down at a four year old version of me, all her joy seeming to seep out of the picture and engulf me.

Grams had said she was overjoyed when I was born, her beauty ethereal because it had been that of a mother's. But in the picture there was a lining about her mouth and eyes that seemed to say more than her smile did. There was something there that belied her happiness, something that made it hard for her to truly bask in the warmth of motherhood. And I didn't know what that could be.

I sighed, picking up the picture to gently place a kiss on my mother's face, tears welling in my eyes. Grams said she'd died of a rare sickness that couldn't be diagnosed. I barely remembered her.

I replaced the picture and moved to my four poster bed with its plush and silky bedding. I couldn't handle thinking of my mother or my Grams now and instead would rather dream of silliness and wishful fantasies.

I undressed and pulled on a long t-shirt and brushed my hair before braiding it and throwing it over one shoulder. Then I burrowed beneath the covers and slowly drifted off, my mind running wild with questions and pictures of beautiful emerald eyes.

Three

I SAT AT the back of the class, resting my head against my forearm, too tired to really pay attention to my biology teacher Mrs. Steely. She was rambling on and on about frogs and dissection and anatomy. It was early morning and this was my first class and it didn't seem right to talk about things like the anatomy when everyone had just woken up.

"Grace Moore." Her voice made me jump and I looked up in time to see everyone turning to look at me and Mrs. Steely's beady eyes narrowing which they often did when she singled me out. "Are you listening to me?"

"Sure am, dissection, anatomy and frogs."

Several kids coughed to cover their laughter and her black eyes burned with fury. "Are you being smart with me Grace?"

"Of course not," I smiled at her. "But I don't know why we would be dissecting frogs this early in the morning."

"Are you questioning me?"

"Yes ma'am."

Silence descended and I fought the urge to roll my eyes. Mrs. Steely just looked at me, obviously at a loss for words for the first time all year. She bent behind the counter and pulled up six jars, each filled with an ugly little frog. I felt like gagging.

I raised my hand and the look I received from Mrs. Steely should have made me combust, if a single look good do such a thing. I smiled at her. "May I be excused?"

"Why?"

"Because I had breakfast today and I don't think everyone wants to see what, exactly, I ate."

"Excuse me?"

"It's nine o'clock in the morning and I don't want to cut open a frog and poke around its insides." I said, my smile vanishing and my eyes narrowing.

Her beady eyes met my glare, hatred gleaming in their blackened depths. Mrs. Steely didn't like me because she, like everyone else in Genevieve, had heard rumours that I and everyone in my family were witches. She also didn't particularly like being called out in front of her class, by me or any other student.

"I didn't ask you what you wanted to do Grace. I'm telling you that we're dissecting frogs as part of the curriculum and you will do as I ask."

I gave her my most vicious smile, the anger bubbling up inside me was almost at boiling point. "You will *not* tell me what to do Mrs. Steely."

It was her turn to smile evilly. "I *am* your elder and teacher Miss Moore, I will tell you what you can and cannot do."

The class was silent as Mrs. Steely watched me, gauging my reaction. At first I didn't react because I didn't have any self control and was close to getting myself expelled. But, thankfully, I didn't need to reply.

All at once there was an incredible popping noise and the jars in the front of the class exploded, spraying glass and formaldehyde across the room. High pitched screams rang throughout the room but no one moved, not even

Mrs. Steely, and it didn't take a genius to know where each person's mind was at that moment and whose name kept repeating inside their heads.

As if they were of one mind, each and every person turned in excruciatingly slow motion to look at me with horrorstruck faces; their eyes wide and their mouths agape. I didn't know what to do or say, I couldn't deny what they'd seen or say that it hadn't been me because it would be stupidity on my part and they never would have believed it, mostly because they knew it wasn't true. I'd destroyed those jars as easily as I'd yelled at our teacher and I was just as surprised as they were.

I stood slowly, feeling their eyes follow my every movement as if they were waiting for me to hurt them.

I picked up my bag and turned to the door without looking at anyone. Someone cleared their throat and out of habit I turned to see those beady eyes watching me again, something like victory gleaming in their depths. "Don't even think about coming back here Witch."

I didn't respond, just turned and ran from the room and out of the school without a backwards glance.

*   *   *

I ran until I was safely on my property and the wrought iron gate banged closed behind me. I leaned against it; out of breath and so close to tears it scared me. I hadn't cried since the day my mother died and I didn't plan to now.

Grams was standing on the porch by the time I picked my way across the pebbled walkway. Her eyes were hard but understanding, a rare mixture for her. "Gray," she didn't ask what had happened and I knew she already knew. But I couldn't form words so I just met her eyes before dropping them to my feet.

"Come inside." she said quietly, her gaze flitting behind me like it often did, in search of danger I had no doubt.

I moved into the foyer and dropped my bag near the wide marble staircase and moved into the living room. I stopped dead, my jaw hanging somewhere near my collar bone.

His smile was just as enchanting as it had been the night before and his eyes were twinkling with mischief and something darker. "Gray," he stood and I backed away slightly.

Grams came in behind me, her eyes hardening at the casual use of my name. "You told him your name?" she snarled, sounding more like a harpy than a grandmother.

I rolled my eyes. "You brought him here?"

He smiled, "I came to see you actually."

"Why?"

A shadow passed over his face but his smile remained. "I was intrigued and wanted to know if my hunch was correct."

"What hunch?"

Grams frowned at him, "Grace this is Lucian McCormick. He's an old friend."

"Of yours?" I laughed despite the tension. "You don't have friends Grams."

"Not of mine." She said softly, her eyes falling to her feet for the first time since I'd been alive. Grams was the kind of woman who could call you the worst names while meeting your gaze unflinchingly, it was completely uncharacteristic of her to drop her eyes.

"Then whose?"

He met my gaze, "Yours actually."

A bark of surprised laughter bubbled out of my throat and sent me on a coughing fit. "What?"

"We knew each other as kids."

"I doubt that, I would have remembered you."

He grinned. "Ah, but I remember you love."

"When were we friends?"

My eyes fell on Grams who was still looking at her socks. "Lucian's mother was Morgana's best friend."

Silence filled the air and my heart skipped a beat. Mom's name was forbidden and Grams had started enforcing that rule as soon as we were back from the graveyard the day of her funeral. I swallowed, my eyes finding Lucian's again. "What?"

"Maybe you should sit down."

"Don't tell me what to do." I snapped, "What's going on? What are you doing here? When the hell were we friends?"

He let out a breath while he ran a hand through unruly black hair. "You were three and I was five, our mothers would stick us together while they sat and drank tea and gossiped. We played in your backyard everyday for a year. And when mom wanted to go back to Ireland, she asked Morgana to come with her, start anew, but your mom refused."

"Why?"

"She said she couldn't take you away from your father."

My breath caught in my throat and I was certain I was going to choke to death. "Don't be ridiculous, my father left when I was born."

13

Gram shifted her feet and my eyes were drawn to the movement. "No he didn't."

I moved into the living room and sank onto the couch opposite Lucian's, my hand on my heart as if that could stifle the incredible pain that seemed to burn within my veins. "He didn't?"

"Your father was around for the first four years of your life." Grams whispered. "He disappeared after Morgana died."

I gasped in air, trying to bring oxygen into my starving lungs. My whole life had been odd just because I lived in the twenty first century in a town ruled by the past but now everything I'd known and grown up knowing was being challenged by a gorgeous stranger I'd only just met the night before.

"What do you mean by disappeared?"

"He left." she said, finally meeting my questioning gaze. "He said he couldn't look at you because you looked too much like Morgana."

My throat felt like it was closing up, I gulped in air like I'd never felt it inside my lungs before now. I was so close to hyperventilating I was sure I was going to pass out. My eyes went back to Lucian who was staring at his hands and skillfully avoiding meeting my eyes. "Is there more?"

"Yes actually, I have a message for the two or you." his eyes flew to Grams and then back to me. "The Hunt is beginning; you must get out before it's too late."

My brows furrowed in confusion but when my eyes fell on Grams fear tightened my heart. She knew what the message meant and it frightened her, my grandmother, the warrior. "Who told you this?"

"Another old friend," Lucian replied, obviously unwilling to divulge any information other than what was necessary. "But I know it's legitimate."

Grams masked her fear with a glare that deserved a standing ovation. "And how can we trust your word Lucian? I haven't seen you since you were six."

He shrugged, his eyes so full of cocky superiority that recognition hit so suddenly it almost took my breath away. With vivid clarity I remembered the freckly faced boy from my childhood, the one I'd hated because he'd forced me to eat a wriggling worm and I'd thrown up all day afterward. Mom had told me that's how boys showed they liked girls and to just do whatever he did to me back to him. I remember hitting him in the nose and making him cry, I had felt victorious until he'd hit me back.

As if he could read my thoughts Lucian smiled widely, winking for effect. "Is that everything *Luke* or is there more?" My voice was so snippy I half expected Grams to scold me.

His eyes narrowed. "You remember me now." It wasn't a question but I couldn't help the nod that followed or the grin that spread across my face; he'd always hated when I called him Luke, but I didn't care, I'd hated him the whole time we'd played together.

"Oh yeah," I replied. "And I want to know who told you to give us this message."

"I can't say." his frown was uncharacteristic but I could see in his eyes he was telling the truth.

"Did you see the person?"

"Of course." his eyes narrowed with indignation. "But I can't tell you, I'm sure you'll find out soon enough anyway."

He stood again, yet another smile spreading across that impossibly handsome face of his. "It's time I take my leave. It was lovely to see you again Grace." He shot me one of his cocky grins and my eyes narrowed.

"Goodbye Luke, it was a splendid visit." I did a very bad version of his accent but got my point across all the same, I even did an internal jig when his smile vanished completely.

"Goodbye Gwen." He said to Grams and she nodded in response. Without saying another word Lucian left, closing the door softly behind him.

I leaned against the back of the couch, closing my eyes. With his visit Lucian had brought a frightening message and information I'd never known I needed. I had a father, somewhere out there, and I didn't remember his face or his name.

"Grace," Grams said softly. I opened my eyes to see the hardness gone from her face for the first time since mom had died. "Do you want to talk?"

"About how I've had a father for the last fifteen years and no one told me? Sure let's start with that."

"His name was John and in his own way he loved Morgana. But he couldn't be here; he left you with me because he had to, because I wouldn't let him take you away with him."

"What? But you said it was because I looked like Mom."

She nodded, "That's partly true but more than that was the fact that he wanted to leave town and take you with him. I couldn't let him."

"Why not?"

"Because Morgana asked me to take care of you no matter what and she told me to never let John have you."

Grams let out a shaky breath and for the first time in my life I realized she wasn't the hard ass I'd grown to know and that she was not impervious to emotion, though she put on a good show.

"Why not Grams?"

She met my eyes for the briefest of moments and the pain I saw there hurt me to my core. "Because Grace, Johnathan Hathorne is a witch hunter."

Four

I EXHALED SLOWLY so that I wouldn't hyperventilate again. Grams was so still I was worried she'd stopped breathing. I ran my hand through my hair, feeling shaky and more than a little afraid.

"My father is a witch hunter?" I whispered.

Grams nodded, "Morgana didn't know until much later."

"How much later?"

"After she found out she was pregnant."

"Did he kill her?"

Grams bit her lip and her gaze fell away from mine. I didn't need her words to know the answer, yes my father had killed my mother, and if Lucian's message was legit my father was coming for me next.

"And The Hunt, what is that exactly?"

When her eyes met mine again there were tears welling there. "The last Hunt was two hundred and thirty years ago when Cadence O'Connell was burned in the town square. And even though it's been a long time since the last one that doesn't mean that it can't happen at any time."

"So you're saying it's like the witch trials of the seventeenth century?" I whispered, more than a little fear seeping into my voice.

Grams sighed. "Yes Gray. But John Hathorne is worse than you can possibly imagine. He's the head Hunter and the most vicious of them all."

"Great," I said more sarcastically than I'd meant to. "What are we going to do?"

"We're going to lie low, you're going to stay inside for a few days and then I'm going to see if I can get you back into school. We're not going to draw anymore unwanted attention to ourselves." She gave me a pointed look.

"I didn't blow up those jars on purpose Grams; I don't even know *how* I did it."

Grams smiled but it was strained and made her look older than she was. "I know that Gray and that's why I'm going to give you something that should help you with your magick."

Oh goody, "What is it?"

"Come with me." She stood and I followed her out of the room and through the hall and down a set of carpeted cement steps that led into our beautifully furnished basement. A grand piano sat in the center of the room with an expensive carpet running along the floor. At the very back of the room was a floor-to-ceiling bookcase and a plush lounge chair in the one corner. Grams went directly to the bookcase where she pulled out a black leather book and handed it to me. The cover was beautiful, with intricate roses lining the edge and a silky red page marker sticking out of the top.

"What's this?"

"This is Cadence O'Connell's Book of Shadows." Grams said softly, stroking the cover tenderly. A Book of Shadows is a witch's journal and a place to record spells and potions. The fact that Grams had Cadence's was weird, because she was the only real witch during the witch trials to be burned at the stake.

"Why do you have it?"

"Because Cadence O'Connell is our ancestor and the first witch in our line." Grams smiled at my wide-eyed expression. "Don't looked so shocked Gray, why do you think people in this town think we're witches in the first place? Most people know that we're related to Cadence and they know the story as well as I do."

"She was burned at the stake in the town square right?"

"Yes, but she was burned by her own brother." Grams said, her smile vanishing. "He was a Hunter and when he found out she was a witch, a real witch, he tied her to a stake and burned her in front of the entire town."

I frowned. "Her brother killed her because she was a witch and he was a Hunter?"

"I don't know the exact reasons behind her death and neither do most of the people in Genevieve but you should be able to piece it together after reading her Book."

"Have you ever read this?"

She smiled but shook her head. "I couldn't bear to read it Gray. I know many people went through a lot of torture and I couldn't read about our ancestor's pain." Grief flicked across her face, almost too fast to catch. "But you're stronger than me, you'll go far Gray."

"No one's stronger than you Grams." I whispered, irrational fear making my insides grow cold at her words. "What's going on?"

She smiled wistfully. "Don't you worry about anything Grace, just go read and I'll take care of everything."

I didn't know what to say so I did as she asked; I retraced my steps and then climbed the huge marble stairs to my room. It was barely noon and already I felt like going to sleep. I wished the day would just end already, I even wished I could wake up and everything would just be an elaborate dream. But I knew this wasn't a dream and that everything was going to change.

I sighed as I sank onto my plush bed and opened Cadence's book:

> *1624, May 24*
>
> *Father has taken ill and mother is in a panic. She's been setting up date after date for a suitable man for me, I've disliked every one. Insufferable, boorish snobs, each and every one. But she says we are losing money quickly because of father's illness and if we don't find me a rich man then we will become peasants. She makes it sound as if peasantry is something akin to the plague.*
>
> *Little John is angry that he's being ignored so often but I tell him that it's better than being treated like a prize to be won, I don't think he is convinced.*
>
> *I hope that mother gives up this delusions of my marrying the men she seems to fancy. Father will be fine and if he is not then at least he will be in a better place. That is what I hold on to now.*
>
> *-C.C*

I frowned at the paper, another John? Was that name really that common? Maybe back then, and maybe it was a coincidence that his name was in Cadence's book. But there was a nagging voice in the back of my mind, reminding me that there was no such thing as coincidence. And Grams had said that Cadence's brother had killed her because he was a Hunter and she was a witch.

But that had been two hundred and thirty years ago; how could John Hathorne, my father, remind me so much of a man who lived in the seventeenth century? It was there, the answer, nagging my thoughts, but I couldn't seem to reach it and I was kind of glad. There was too much danger in my life now, and a new revelation would only make it that much worse.

I set Cadence's book on the nightstand and dropped back onto my pillow. Too many thoughts flitted through my mind and I couldn't for the life of me make sense of them. The nagging feeling was getting worse the longer I ignored the thoughts about my father and the secrets Mom and Grams had kept from me, but I did my best to ignore it as I closed my eyes and drifted asleep.

I dreamt that night.

The sky was a frightening blood red as the sun sank below the horizon. The smell of fire filled the air and the sound of a thousand impatient people was almost thick enough to cut through. I sat in a cold and smelly dungeon. An ugly brown dress covered me from neck to ankles, hiding the worst of the bruises and slashes; my hair was unmanageably long and caked with blood.

A man stood outside the door, his face covered in shadows. He was silent, his eyes boring into mine as I forced myself to meet them, though I could not see them. He didn't move for a long time and a small part of me hoped he'd changed his mind.

"Are you ready?" The voice was as familiar to me as my own but now held no tenderness, no joy, it was an emotionless approximation of the voice I'd grown up with and the difference hurt me to my core.

I didn't respond just stood, holding my head high despite the thick whip lashes that screamed in protest from their place across my back. Keys jingled as he opened my cage door, moving aside to let me pass. I walked steadily, purposely ignoring the intense pain vying for my attention; these lacerations were fresh and still so very painful, but I would not allow them the satisfaction of knowing such a thing.

John followed close at my back, his steps silent on the cold stone. I ignored the prickling sensation of his eyes boring into the back of my skull, he would not get a rise out of me, nor would he burrow his way into my mind and force a confession from my lips.

We moved up the stone steps without a word and men with shackles moved out of the shadows to clasp the cold metal to my wrists and ankles. I was led out by the chain that held the shackles together, feeling like a dog on a leash.

When we moved into the cold air there were applause and goading cheers. But I ignored the booing and the jeering as I made my way across the wooden platform to where a stake protruded out of the hole cut in the wood. Beneath the platform was kindling, leaning against the bottom of the stake. The idea of burning frightened me, I'd always harbored a fear of fire and now I knew why.

John stopped at a podium, his eyes roving over the crowd, too afraid to meet my gaze. The men who'd shackled me brought me to stand in front of the stake, turning me so I faced the crowd before they unshackled me and replaced my bonds with rope, wrapping it around the thick wooden stake until my back was pressed against my pyre.

Silence descended on us all and my heart beat quickened, but I kept my face impassive and my eyes burning with righteous indignation as I surveyed the crowd, many of whom I recognized. John cleared his throat and all eyes turned to him, mine followed, out of habit.

"Cadence O'Connell, you stand accused of witchcraft, how do you plea?" John asked, his eyes meeting mine for the first time without the mask of shadows; they were the same intense blue my father had and they were full of regret and something more, something sinister.

I realized then that it was too late for my brother.

"I did not harm those children Johnathan Hathorne but I am what you say." I exhaled as the crowd erupted, jeering and hissing.

"For how long, dearest sister, have you been a witch?"

I met his gaze unflinchingly, my own golden eyes filling with unstoppable tears; John was my twin but he would see me burn over something as petty as not being Chosen by the Goddess. "All of my life." I answered.

"For how long have you been working for the devil?"

"I do not work for Satan; there is no Satan in witchcraft." But my words were only met with more hissing. These people could not understand and it was because of power hungry men like my brother. I felt pity for them and the world in which they lived.

"Why did you hurt those children?"

"I did not."

"Do not lie. Tillie said she saw you that night."

"I gave Tillie a poultice for a bruise she received while walking the street to bring her mother baked goods. I did not harm her."

My words fell on deaf ears and a chant began, softly at first but then became a scream, a scream for my death. They wanted me to burn; they were tired of my lies. I looked my brother in the eyes, knowing I would not beg for my life but knowing also that he did not want me dead.

A torch was passed down the crowd and handed to John; he moved to stand in front of me, blocking my view of the townspeople. His hard eyes changed, softened and his mask fell away until my brother was standing before me with pleading eyes.

"Just give me what I want Cade and I will let you go." he whispered, his words drowned out by the horrid chanting.

"It doesn't work that way John, I'm not trying to hurt you or make you angry, but you were not Chosen. There is nothing I can do."

I watched with morbid fascination as my brother disappeared only to be replaced by Judge Johnathan Hathorne. His cold blue eyes bore into mine, "You have chosen your fate Cadence O'Connell. May you burn in hell."

And without blinking an eye my brother dropped the torch at my feet and I went up in an agony of fire.

Five

I woke up screaming. Grams ran into my room, brandishing the broom as a weapon; her eyes wild and her hair flying. "Grace what is it?"

I sat up, my scream dying as tears spilled from my eyes and I was sobbing hard into my hands. I heard the broom clatter to the floor as Grams half ran to my side, pulling me into her embrace. She rocked me back and forth while she whispered sweet things into my ear.

When I could breathe again and the tears had subsided I moved my hands from my face and looked up at my Grams. "It was horrible." I whispered the dream replaying even as I spoke. "I was in so much pain."

"Why? What did you dream?"

"I dreamt of my death." I whispered, "But I wasn't me, I was Cadence."

I watched as her eyes fell on Cadence's Book and a frown creased her face. "You shouldn't read that before you go to bed Gray."

I rolled my eyes. "I only read the first page."

We were silent. For the first time in my life Grams had no soothing words to offer me on the first occasion since my mom died that I truly needed them.

It was almost unheard of for a witch to dream of an ancestor unless it was a past-life. And even then it was ridiculously rare to have a past-life experience. I couldn't know for sure if it had been a past-life but if it had been just an astral projection I would have been nothing but an observer.

"It's six, would you like breakfast?"

I doubted I would be able to digest anything but I nodded anyway. Grams helped me stand and we moved silently through the hallway and down the marble staircase. I sat at the dining table, my fingers automatically tracing the perfect circles made naturally in the wood as I listened to Grams move around in the kitchen.

There was a small part of me that wished I was still powerless and ignorant to some of the secrets in my life. It had been an easier life and, now, the longer I went on knowing things I hadn't before the more frightening truths I uncovered. It wasn't all that pleasant.

Suddenly, I grabbed a black sharpie from the bowl in the center of the table. Whiteness filled my mind and I stared at the perfect circles I'd been tracing as my hand moved hurriedly over the tabletop. I couldn't see what was happening or what I was drawing, the whiteness blinded me. But I did hear a sharp intake of breath and the clattering of glass as it shattered on the hardwood.

The sharpie was pulled from my grasp and the whiteness dissolved, I looked up at Grams who was white-faced and wide-eyed. "What?"

But she wasn't looking at me; she was looking at the table. I turned my gaze to the tabletop and my jaw fell open. There, on the perfect mahogany of our tabletop, was an amazingly detailed portrait of a boy around my age. He was cute in a floppy-haired kind of way, his eyes light and intense. His face was familiar and perfectly chiseled; like a younger version of Apollo.

"Who did this?" I asked, knowing the answer as soon as the words left my mouth. "No way, we only get one power."

Grams was speechless as she stared transfixed at the picturesque drawing of a boy I'd never seen before. "And you dreamt of Cadence." It wasn't a question and I didn't know where she was headed.

"Grams, I couldn't have done this."

She met my eyes, regret and fear vying for dominance in her expression. "This is surprising." She said softly, sinking into the chair beside me, "Go get Cadence's book."

I half ran to my room to retrieve the book before I clattered down the steps. Grams hadn't moved from her spot, her eyes glued to the picture on the table. She didn't hear me when I came in or when I pulled the chair out and it scraped loudly against the hardwood.

"Are you okay Grams?" I whispered, ducking my head so I could meet her eyes.

She didn't smile just held her hand out for the book. She opened it wordlessly, flicking from page to page until she came to a passage that satisfied her, then she pushed the book to me and my gaze fell to the worn pages and the black ink.

1624, June 3

I've discovered something today, something most frightening. I made something explode with just a thought; Mother screamed so loudly I thought the glass in the windows might break.

John and Father were not home and for that I was most grateful, neither of them knows Mother is a practicing witch and that, as the only other woman in our household, it is quite possible that I will be magickal as well. But, when I was fourteen Mother initiated me into the Goddess's circle deep in the heart of the Lion Oak forest where she and eleven other women go to worship their deity.

But, today on my nineteenth birthday, Mother and I got into an argument and all of our bowls and plates burst into pieces. We both screamed and stared at each other with wide fearful eyes.

I asked Mother if she'd done it and she said that the Goddess had not gifted her with magick like that, her power was to make poultices and spells to help others, not to destroy things.

For the rest of the day Mother looked at me as if I'd been marked by Satan himself. It frightens me, this gift she gave me, what if I should hurt someone?

-C.C

I looked up to see Grams watching me, I swallowed thickly. "What does this mean?"

She ignored my question. "There's more."

I turned the page and read some more.

1624, June 25

It's been weeks since I've hidden my thoughts in your protective pages and that is because I no longer feel as if anything is safe. Mother has stopped inviting me to the Goddess Circles because she does not believe my magick stems from the Goddess, she thinks me a demon. No one has questioned her judgment because she is the leader of their circle, her word is law.

Since I blew up our plates and bowls Mother hasn't been in the same room with me for more than a few seconds. And then, yesterday, something else happened.

I was overtaken by this blinding whiteness, my entire mind had gone blank and then, without my volition, my hand had moved over the paper so quickly and surely it was as if I were possessed.

When the whiteness had vanished I was shocked to find the most detailed drawing I'd ever created, and I am not particularly fluent as an artist. It was an amazingly accurate portrait of my dear brother John, but there was a coldness in his eyes that I'd never seen there before.

Mother had come into the room when I was possessed by the whiteness and now more than ever she believes me to be a demon. It is heartbreaking, we have grown so far apart and I know some of the reason is jealousy. Mother has been a loyal practitioner for years and the Goddess never gifted her with magick like mine, I know deep down she knows I am not a demon but a daughter of the Goddess and she resents me for it.

I wish she did not; I miss her so very much.
-C.C

"I have all her powers?" I whispered looking up at Grams as realization struck.

"So far you have two of her powers." Grams corrected, watching me with carefully masked eyes. "And you've been dreaming of her."

"It was only one dream."

"One is enough Grace." Grams sighed and met my eyes again. "And your explosive power, it's rare for our family."

"What do you mean?"

"I mean, Cadence had three major powers. She could make things blow up, draw the future and move things with her mind. The woman in our family only ever got the last two, no one since Cadence has had the explosive power until you and then you received the future one as well. And on top of that you dreamed not of her but as if you were her."

I bit my lip. "What are you saying exactly Grams?"

"I'm saying that you dreamt of Cadence and you got another of her powers. You could very well be her incarnation."

Silence descended as I absorbed her words and our eyes fell on the picture I'd drawn with amazing accuracy. My brows furrowed as I remembered something Cadence had written, I opened the book again until I came to the page after the last entry I'd read.

Judge Johnathan Hathorne looked out at me from the page, the coldness in his eyes almost a mirror image of the look he'd given Cadence before he'd set her aflame. "Grams, have you ever seen this man?" I asked, turning the book around and pushing it towards her.

I watched as her eyes widened and her mouth dropped open. "This can't be." She whispered, touching the picture. "What is this?"

"It's a picture of Cadence's twin brother Johnathan Hathorne." I replied, frowning.

Grams looked as if she'd forgotten how to breathe. "Johnathan Hathorne?"

"Yeah," I remembered when Grams told me about my father, the estranged *John Hathorne*. "Why does he have the same name as my father?"

She met my eyes for the briefest of moments before she turned the picture back around and pushed it towards me, "Because this man is John Hathorne, your father and the most dangerous witch hunter in the world.

Six

"How can that be?" I asked, pacing back and forth in front of Grams. "That would make him over two hundred and thirty years old."

She nodded solemnly. "Yes it would and it would make him an ancestor of ours seeing as he was Cadence's twin brother."

"Isn't that like incest?"

Grams shrugged. "Morgana would have been his great, great, great and so on niece."

My whole body shivered at the idea, I gagged deep in my throat. "Why would he do that? He had to have known we were related to him."

"Unless we weren't."

"What?"

"Well, think about it. Cadence and her mother were witches but Cadence was the only one with magick, true magick. Her mother was jealous and what if John was too? What if he wanted to have magick like his sister? What if he didn't because he wasn't really her twin but an adopted sibling?"

"That's a bit of a leap Grams." I said, running my hand through my nest of tangled hair. "Why would you think he wasn't related to her when she called him her twin?"

"Children are lied to all the time, our family is no different." Grams said quietly. "But if I'm right then your father isn't Cadence's brother, not biologically anyway, which means that his extended life and whatever else he's done are unnatural."

I shook my head at the absurdity of her words though they made plenty of sense. It didn't make sense that Cadence's twin wouldn't be as magickal as her, and if John was her twin then he should have had magic too. But he hadn't and their parents hadn't been magickal either.

"What if you're right about the adoption but wrong about the child?" I said, turning to her, a smile spreading across my face.

"What do you mean?"

"Cadence was the only one in her family who had magick, what if she was the adopted sibling and not John? Her mother had been jealous too, it says so in her journal, what if it was because she became a member of the Goddess Circle only to receive magick and her adoptive child got what she couldn't?"

"It makes much more sense that way."

"I agree."

"Then who are Cadence's real parents?"

I shrugged. "I don't know and I have a feeling John doesn't either."

"Even after two hundred and thirty years?"

I shrugged again. "Cadence didn't know, up to the end she thought he was her brother, her twin, though they looked nothing alike."

"So John could think he was Cadence's brother still and that he wasn't in the Goddess's favour when in fact he was never meant to be magickal because Cadence wasn't his biological sister."

"Exactly," we smiled at each other because we'd figured out a part of the mystery but there was still so much left. Like who was the boy I'd drawn on our tabletop?

I sighed, sinking back into my chair. "What are we going to do if I am Cadence's incarnation? John will come back for me if he thinks there's a chance I could be."

"Except he thought Morgana was."

"What?"

"Yeah, he thought she was Cadence's incarnation."

"Ew," I felt bile rising in my throat. "She was his sister."

"She might not have been."

"But he didn't know that."

Grams nodded, fear and disgust shining in her eyes.

I sighed, completely grossed out and more than a little tired of this conversation. Everything had been kind of normal just yesterday and now everything was different and everything had changed. "I'm going to go for a walk Grams. Don't wait up okay?"

"Grace wait, let's talk."

"We've been talking for hours; I need to think and to do that I need to be alone and far away from here. I'm sorry." I moved into the foyer and pulled on my coat and scarf before stuffing my feet into my boots. I left without a backwards glance, drawing my scarf closer to me.

I moved through the sleeping town, the snow crunching beneath my boots as I walked towards the forest bordering Genevieve. I couldn't stay here in this repressed town where my ancestor had died all those years ago and my life was now spiraling out of control. I needed to go where no one knew my name or my secrets; I needed to go to the closest metropolis, Vase Line.

I ran most of the way through the forest, not stopping to breathe or think. When I cleared the trees I was breathing heavily and there was sweat freezing on my forehead. Vase Line was the complete opposite of Genevieve, while my small town was sleeping this city was bustling with wide-eyed people.

All the shops were open, music and people poured out of pubs along the streets and people waved at one another, stopping to chat and catch up. It was such a difference compared to Genevieve that I welcomed it with open arms.

I moved down the street, avoiding people as they hurried along to shop or drink. I stopped dead suddenly as my eyes fell on a familiar face; he was cute in a floppy-haired kind of way, his eyes an intensely light blue. He was tall but I could see the boyish features fighting for dominance over a slowly maturing face.

I started to backtrack, turning even as I started to run. I didn't get far though; instead I ran face first into someone's hard chest while strong arms moved to encircle me before I fell. I was held until I could regain my balance and then I looked up into laughing emerald eyes.

It was just my luck.

"Luke," I hissed, looking around for the blue-eyed boy who hadn't noticed my very ungraceful moment. I turned back to Lucian, noticing a space between a store and pub in time to push him into it. A seductive smile spread across his face as he misconstrued my intentions and for a second I couldn't even think, it was that enchanting.

"Well now Gray, I never took you for that kind of girl."

"Shut up." I hissed, peeking around the side of the store in search of the blue-eyed boy.

"What are you doing?" Lucian asked, his head poking out above me. "Do you fancy that boy?"

I rolled my eyes, turning to push him back behind the store's wall. "Of course I don't." I snapped, "I don't even know him."

"Then why are you spying on him?"

"I drew him today." I replied, looking back at the boy in question from my hideout, "On my kitchen table."

"Is that some kind of riddle?" He asked a smile in his voice, "Because I don't get it."

I fought the urge to hit him. "You knew my mom could draw the future I presume?"

"You presume correct."

"Well, I did that today." I said quietly. "And I drew that boy's face on our table with a sharpie."

He grinned, "Really? But don't you already have a power?"

I nodded. "I can blow things up."

His eyes lit up at the thought, "Really? I'd like to see that some time."

"Oh I'm sure you will since it only happens when I'm angry."

"Do I bring out the worst in you Gracie?"

I growled in response turning to look for the boy but he'd disappeared. I sighed as I turned back to Lucian in all his grown up glory. He really was marvelous to look at, he'd come along way from the gangly boy I'd spent a year of my childhood avoiding. He was thick with muscle and his face was perfectly even and filled out.

He seemed to enjoy looking at me as much as I enjoyed looking at him; he grinned widely, looking very much like a fox as he did. "Are you hungry love?"

I bit my lip; I didn't want anything to do with Lucian for many reasons, some of which because he'd tortured me when we were kids. But I didn't want to go home and he knew his way around Vase Line better than I did. There couldn't be much harm in having dinner with him, could there?

I shrugged, giving him my best smile. "If you're buying."

He laughed, resting his arm on my shoulders as he steered us out of the alley. He pointed to a quiet, uncluttered restaurant across the street and my stomach rumbled as if in response. He laughed again and we made our way to the restaurant where a pretty hostess smiled at us both. "Table for two." Lucian said, giving her a wink that should have made her melt, I rolled my eyes.

"Right away sir." She said, giving him a shy little giggle before hurrying away.

"You're a pig." I said under my breath.

"You love it." he countered, smiling when the woman returned. She grabbed two menus and motioned for us to follow her into the quiet, candlelit dining area, where couples were smiling and whispering, looking into one another's eyes with all the love in the world. I felt sickeningly out of place.

We were led to a small table in the corner; one side was a padded booth and the other a hard wooden chair. Like the gentleman he certainly was not, Lucian offered me the booth. I could feel the strained smile on my face and sat in time to see the waitress roll her eyes at my lack of gratitude.

"Can I get you anything to drink?" She asked her eyes on Lucian as she addressed the both of us. I rolled my eyes again.

"A pint if you got it love." he said giving her the most devastating smile I've ever seen.

"And for the lady?" She asked icily, dragging her eyes from Lucian long enough to give me a cold look.

I smiled at her, "Coffee."

"I'll be right back."

"Take your time." I said with as much frost as I could muster.

When she walked away Lucian leaned back against his chair the most mischievous grin playing across his luscious lips. "Well, wasn't that entertaining. You know she'll probably spit in your coffee now."

"I'm not all that thirsty anyway." I responded, ignoring his insinuation that I'd behaved in any way like a jealous girlfriend.

"So, what are you doing in Vase Line again this week?"

I shrugged. "I needed out and I couldn't go anywhere in Genevieve without Grams being able to see me. I wanted to breathe." I frowned. "What do you mean again this week?"

For the first time since I'd met him Lucian blushed, ever so slightly, and surprisingly I found it adorable. But he was saved answering for the moment when the waitress returned, setting a tall pint of beer in front of Lucian and a steaming cup of coffee in front of me. I didn't see any spit, I hoped.

"Are you ready to order?" She asked.

Lucian was watching me, no longer interested in the waitress and that gave me an oddly warm feeling in my gut but I ignored it and met her cold eyes. "We need a couples minutes."

"I'll be back." she said vehemently.

Lucian smiled when she was gone. "What are you in the mood for? My treat."

"You bet," I replied, smiling slightly. "But tell me what you meant Lucian."

"About what, love?"

"About my visiting again this week."

He sighed, falling back against the hard wood of his chair. "I've noticed you."

To my disgust my heart fluttered giddily at his words. "What?"

"Whenever you come into Vase Line I'm here, watching you." he frowned, looking into the dark liquid of his Guinness. "I'm not a stalker."

"No, not at all." I said softly, unable to hide my surprise. I wasn't as troubled by this proclamation as I should have been. "How often have you been here when I come into town?"

"Every week for the last year."

I gasped in surprise. "Why did it take you so long to run into me? You don't seem to have any trouble talking to girls."

He smiled but it didn't reach his eyes. "I'm not as brave as I act." he answered. "Besides, I knew you wouldn't recognize me."

"All the more reason to talk to me sooner."

"Did Gwen tell you everything?" he asked.

I shrugged, frowning. "What does that have to do with this?"

"Answer my question Gray."

"I think she did."

He nodded. "If I came to you sooner you would have learned the bad things sooner and I didn't want that responsibility, I still don't. I don't want you to hate me."

"I don't hate you." and I was surprised that these words were true. "This isn't your fault."

"It is, partly."

"What do you mean?"

"I gave you the message, I made it so Gwen had to tell you the things she hadn't. Don't you blame me?"

"Of course not. This isn't because of you. Grams kept things from me because she thought it was best, just because you helped her tell me doesn't mean I blame you."

He smiled the most beautiful smile I'd ever seen in my life. I couldn't help but return it. "I'm glad."

"Good," I could feel my cheeks burning beneath his blatant gaze so I ducked my head and my eyes found the menu. "Should we order?"

"Yes, of course."

We perused the menu and Lucian ordered fries and a burger and I got a chicken pot pie with fries on the side. We ate in silence for a long time, both of us lost in our own thoughts.

"Can you only do compulsion?" I asked him around a mouthful of chicken and gravy.

He shrugged. "It's not my main gift if that's what you're asking." I nodded for him to continue as I took another big bite. "Compulsion runs in my family, every one of us has it. My main power is the ability to read emotions."

"Emotions? Wouldn't that make you an Empath?"

He nodded, "Its part of the reason why my compulsion is so strong."

"Isn't Empathy hard? Can't it drive you crazy?"

He shrugged. "I've had it since I was fourteen; I've learned to control it."

I nodded. "Can I ask you something?"

"Shoot," he bit into his burger, his eyes never leaving my face.

"Who gave you the message?"

"Why do you want to know?"

"I asked first."

He sighed, returning his burger to its plate. "Do you remember the boy you were hiding from?"

"Yes?"

"He and I have known each other for quite some time. He told me of The Hunt and we were meeting today but you sidetracked me."

"You were supposed to meet him? Why?"

He shrugged. "He wanted to tell me something."

"Why aren't you there? Aren't you curious?"

He smiled and there was something odd in his eyes when he looked at me. "I'd much rather be here having dinner with you. We're practically on a date you know."

I scoffed. "Let's not get ahead of ourselves Luke. I barely know you. One year of childhood trauma doesn't mean we're destined to be."

He smiled. "How could you know that?"

"I just do. Why don't we go meet this guy?"

"No," he said, shaking his head, all the teasing gone from his voice and expression. "I don't want you anywhere near this guy."

"Why?"

"Because. Let's just finish eating and I'll take you home."

"Don't tell me what to do Lucian." I snarled. "Why won't you introduce me to this guy?"

"He's dangerous Gray, just leave it alone."

"How could he be dangerous, have you seen him?"

He sighed, running a hand through hair. "His name is Connor Hathorne and he's the son of the infamous John Hathorne, your father."

My heart almost stopped beating. "What?"

"Yeah, he's your brother."

I barely heard him as I stood, his brows furrowed as a frown creased his mouth. "What's wrong Gray?"

"Grams," I whispered, moving towards the door. Lucian threw money on the table, far too much for our meager meal, and followed me out of the restaurant, my coat in his arms.

"What about her Gray?" He asked, turning me to face him as he draped my coat over my shoulders.

"He's come for her; we have to get to Genevieve."

"What are you talking about Grace?"

I looked into his perfect emerald eyes as my worst fear came to life and my heart felt as if it might break. "John Hathorne is starting The Hunt and he's going to start it with Grams. He's going to kill her."

Seven

"WHAT ARE YOU talking about?" Lucian asked, holding me by the tops of my arms to keep me upright. "How can you know this?"

"I just do, we need to go now."

"Okay, are you sure?"

I shook my head, "But I think I know who will be."

"Who?"

"Connor," I looked into his reluctant emerald eyes. "We don't have time to argue about this Luke, you need to take me to Connor. Please?"

I don't know if it was the fear in my eyes or the fear in my voice but Lucian didn't argue, just took my hand and led me through the still-crowded streets of Vase Line to a small pub where he was supposed to meet Connor. There were only a few people inside but we saw Connor instantly, sitting at the back of the room, a beer in front of him, his eyes fixed on us.

We went to sit at his table and we both ordered a beer though I couldn't have drank it if I'd wanted to with the knots tightening within my gut. Connor assessed me quietly, showing no emotion on his face or in his eyes.

"I asked you to meet me alone Lucian." Connor said quietly.

"I wasn't going to come here Connor, but there's something we have to ask you."

"We?" He looked at me again, his blue eyes cold. "Who is this?"

"This is Grace Moore." Lucian said softly. "Your sister."

"I know who Grace Moore is." Connor snapped the first real emotion I'd seen in him since we sat down. "What's she doing here?"

"Hello? I'm sitting right here." I said angrily, "I asked Luke to bring me to you because I drew you this morning and I know you know what's going on now and where your father is. Did he go to Genevieve?"

"Why would you ask that?"

"Because if he came back then he went after Grams and me if he thought I was still there. I need to know if he went to Genevieve, please, you have to tell me."

Connor blew out a breath and looked at Lucian. "You gave them the message?"

"Yes," Lucian answered his eyes on my face.

Connor met my gaze. "He went to Genevieve tonight, that's why I asked Lucian to meet me here, so I could get him to warn you and Gwen."

My heart clenched. "Warn us about what?" but I knew, I didn't need his confirmation. John had returned to kill off our line and I'd left Grams alone and vulnerable. I had enough magick to fight by her side and I'd left to come to Vase Line. I was safe but Grams was in incredible danger.

I stood without waiting for Connor's reply and I ran from the pub, through the streets, pushing people out of my way in my haste to get into the forest. I ran until my lungs burned and I felt like dropping dead from exhaustion and still I ran on. I only stopped when I came to the edge of the forest that overlooked Genevieve.

The sky was red and the air was thick with smoke. There was screaming, people were awake, staring wide eyed out their windows. In the center of town, visible at any angle of Genevieve, was my house, the beautiful four hundred year old Victorian manor that my family had lived in for generations and it was ablaze.

I sobbed at the sight and started to run for it, but I was caught in mid-air by a familiar set of strong arms. I fought and clawed and screamed, all to no avail. Lucian had a good hold on me and there was no getting out of it. The people of Genevieve watched my house burn and listened to my grandmother scream and not one person went to her aid, not one person moved from their house or their spot on the street.

A deep hatred burned in my veins as I looked at each of the people I'd grown to know in my nineteen years of life. They were horrible people, each too self centered to lend a helping hand, and people wanted the small town life for its charm. When I looked out on Genevieve that night I saw no charm, just ignorant, selfish people, watching an old lady burn. Lucian dragged me from the edge of the forest, pulling me into his arms and resting my head against his chest. He whispered words I couldn't hear, trying to soothe my tears and my aching heart.

My whole body shook with the force of my sobbing, I couldn't think, I couldn't feel anything but an intense grief and a burning anger. I wanted so badly to run into that house and save her, I wanted to bring her out and heal her, I wanted to kill Johnathan Hathorne for hurting her and killing my ancestor. I wanted to hate Lucian for holding me back, but I didn't and I knew I couldn't.

After a while Lucian lifted me up and carried me away. A long time passed but I was too tired and sad to note the route we were taking. When we finally stopped I lifted my head and was shocked to see a small house, almost a shack it was so ramshackle, standing alone beside a stream. Connor sat outside, his face grim, his eyes still as cold as ever.

I twisted in Lucian's grip until he let me go and then I launched myself at Connor, clawing and screaming as rage consumed me. I could hear the most amazing cracking sound, as if someone had hit a tree with a Mack truck. And then, suddenly, just as Lucian grabbed me off of Connor three trees exploded, showering us in wood splinters, and splashing the biggest pieces into the river beside the house.

Silence descended, Connor had a long gash across his cheek but it wasn't deep and it barely bled. He put his hand over it as he stared at me with a mixture of amazement and horror. As if we were being controlled by the same puppet master all three of us turned to look at the trees that had lined the opposite side of the river, there was nothing but thick, sharp stumps remaining, what was left of the trees lay across the river or was splintered along the snow.

"Gray?" Lucian turned me so I had to look at him, his beautiful eyes so full of tenderness and sorrow that it made my heart ache even more. "Are you okay?"

"No," I replied, my voice barely a whisper. "I'm the farthest thing from okay." I turned to look at Connor who was still staring transfixed at what was left of those trees. "We could have left; we could have saved her, if only he'd stopped playing games and told us that his father had gone to Genevieve."

Connor looked at me, his eyes narrowing. "First of all he's your father too and second, if I hadn't delayed you, you would be in that house burning with your grandmother. Do you really believe she would have wanted that? Do you really think she wouldn't have sent you away too?"

"Why should you care if I burn? You're a hunter just like your father."

"I am, but not by choice."

"What does that mean?"

"It doesn't matter now. I care because half of your blood is the same half that runs in my veins. You're my sister and I won't let you die."

I was shocked. "But you're a product of Johnathan Hathorne."

"You make it sound like he manufactured me."

"I just mean he's evil and you grew up with him, so you should be that way too."

He smiled sadly, a tortured soul lying imprisoned within his bright blue eyes. "There are many things about our father that you do not know. But I won't go into detail now, when I come back in two weeks I'll tell you what I can. In the meantime stay here with Lucian; he's your only ally now."

He spoke as if we were at war and in a sad way I knew it was true; Johnathan Hathorne had managed to live for two centuries by a means I had yet to learn and he hated my family because of Cadence and the fact that he hadn't been chosen by the Goddess to wield magick. This war was a long time coming and it would begin with one of the strongest witches in the world, Gwendolyn Moore, my Grams.

But now, with Grams dead, I was the last of the Moore witches and the strongest since Cadence. But I didn't feel any elation at the thought, all I could think was I wasn't ready and Grams could have done this. She'd been the strongest woman I'd ever known and now she was gone and if she could be killed then I could be too and I was afraid to die.

"Yes, all right." I said, too tired to argue and too afraid to say what I really felt, that I was afraid of John Hathorne. I was afraid to die and more than that I was afraid to lose any more people to Hathorne and his Hunters.

"That's enough for one night." Lucian said, stepping between Connor and me. He took my hand and nodded to Connor before he turned to me, leading me to his house.

"I'll be back." I turned in time to see Connor's blue eyes before he walked into the darkness of the surrounding forest.

I followed Lucian inside, ignoring the nagging feeling in my stomach; the one that was trying to tell me what was going on, what Hathorne had become and what in turn he'd made Connor and me. Lucian led me down a hallway where a bedroom was sandwiched between a guest room and a bathroom. He took me to the bed and helped me onto it, pulling off my shoes and coat before helping me beneath the covers. Then he sat beside me on the bed, his beautiful emerald eyes glowing in the light of the moon spilling in from the window.

"Would you like to talk Gray?" he whispered, running a finger tip along the side of my face. It felt so good that I smiled.

"I'm sad," I whispered, hating the way my voice cracked. "And I'm afraid."

Lucian touched my lips with his finger, his eyes shining down at me. "I am too, love. But I'll be here; I won't let anything happen to you. I swear it."

I smiled again but it hurt my heart to hear those words. I didn't want Lucian to put his life on the line for me; I didn't want him to die because of me or my family. "Don't say that." I whispered. "You can't protect me, this is my fight and I need to beat Hathorne. You need to live and stay safe, that's what I want you to do for me."

Lucian didn't say anything and I knew he wouldn't agree to that. It bothered me that he cared so much, that he'd been watching me, that he remembered me from our childhood. Because that meant that he'd been thinking of me for all these years and that he felt things for me that I'd never known in my life, things that would only get dangerous now that we were being Hunted.

"Go to sleep Gray, I'll be here when you wake up."

I didn't have any words for him, my mind had forgotten how to work, so I did what he asked, I fell asleep and it was a blissfully dreamless night.

Eight

WHEN I WOKE I was still so exhausted. My eyes stung from crying, my body hurt from running and my heart was in a million pieces and rested somewhere near my stomach. At first I didn't know where I was, the room was bright and colourful, and the bed was so comfortable it almost dragged me back into blissful unconsciousness. The window was large and the curtains were thrown open, revealing a brilliant day.

And then there was Lucian, he was sitting in a chair at the side of my bed, a blanket draped over his body, his beautiful eyes closed. He didn't snore but I could tell he was sleeping and that he wasn't having a dreamless sleep like I'd been lucky enough to have. I could tell by the slant of his mouth and the tightening of his muscles that his dream was bad.

I threw off the covers and moved to his side, resting my knees on the hardwood floor as I looked up into his face. I wanted to wake him but I was afraid to, I knew there was something you weren't supposed to wake people up from. Was it nightmares or night terrors?

"Luke," I whispered.

His head moved towards my voice but his eyes didn't open. I heard him whimper softly and I made up my mind, I stood and leaned over him, resting my hand on his shoulder before I shook him hard. He didn't wake, his eyes didn't even flutter. I put my other hand on his other shoulder and shook with all my strength but he still wouldn't wake.

"Luke, wake up." I said louder now, putting my face inches from his. "Luke!"

He stirred, seeming to like my voice. I frowned, "I'm cooking Luke, and I think I set the stove on fire."

His lips twitched but he still didn't wake. I was growing anxious and I was afraid that this dream would hurt him, I was afraid that it was something he'd been reliving and couldn't get past, something that no doubt had to do with our mothers.

I looked at his face, so beautiful, even when he looked frightened. His eyes roved beneath his eyelids, his hair was messy and hung around his handsome face in slight curls. His lips were so luscious and soft-looking that I remembered when I saw him in Vase Line the day before last, I'd thought them kissable.

I bit my lip as I fought to keep my smile at bay. This was a very good excuse to kiss him, even if it was taking advantage. But I had a feeling he wouldn't complain, even if he woke up during.

I made up my mind in an instant, partly because I couldn't pass up an opportunity to kiss someone as gorgeous as Lucian, even if I wouldn't admit it aloud. So I bent my head, resting my hands on his shoulders, and I dropped my lips to his. At first there was no reaction from him, he was still asleep, but as my eyes closed I saw his open briefly before he parted his lips, kissing me with so much passion it took my breath away.

His arms came around me, pulling me into his lap as my hands found his face. I pulled him closer, kissing him as hard and passionately as I knew how. I'd been right; his lips were soft and more than kissable. He knew how to kiss and he did it with such authority that it made my whole body tingle and my legs feel like wet noodles.

We pulled apart, our eyes locking, emerald and gold. He gave me a tender smile, "What was that for?"

I smiled despite myself. "I couldn't wake you normally."

"Well that's definitely one way to do it." he grinned and this time lust heated his eyes.

"Well you were deeply asleep." I said, a blush burning my cheeks, "and you were just sitting there looking all kissable."

"Was I?" he smiled, tightening his hold on me. "I should learn what that looks like so I can get you to kiss me while I'm awake and alert."

I grinned. "It didn't take you long to be awake and alert."

"You're very right." he smiled, his eyes moving over my face as he searched for something, but he didn't look satisfied when his eyes met mine. "You're still tired."

The statement shocked me because it was such a change in topic. "So what?"

"Did you dream?"

"No, did you?"

"Yes," he frowned and reluctance passed over his features.

"What was it about?"

"Nothing of consequence."

"I don't believe you."

He shrugged, "Believe what you want."

"Was it about our mothers?" I didn't know how I knew but I could see in his eyes that I'd struck a nerve.

"Please don't Gray." he whispered, resting his chin on my shoulder. His voice was so sad, his eyes so full of hurt, that I listened to him for the first time since we'd met. I let it go.

But I realized I was still on his lap and I was suddenly freaked out by the closeness. I untangled myself from him and stood, stretching and yawning as I moved away from him. He stood too, pretending it didn't bother him that I was no longer sitting there, and went to the door. I followed him into the living room where there were two couches facing one another and a coffee table in between.

"Are you hungry?" He asked.

"Not really," I replied. I couldn't eat when I was upset and the longer I was awake the more my mind went to Grams and our house and the fact that I hadn't been there to save her. My heart ached and I put my hand over it, turning my tear-filled eyes to the window.

"Grace?"

"What Luke?"

"Would you like a shower?"

I turned to him, his eyes knowing and sad, not a hint of sarcasm in his voice or expression. A shower, hot water and time alone, it sounded downright blissful. "Please," I whispered, standing to follow him down the hall and into the room to the right of his bedroom. He pulled out two fluffy white towels from the cupboard beside the wide glass shower and placed them on the toilet's lid.

The only thing I found out of place in his bathroom was the lack of a bathtub. The only thing I could use to clean myself was the glass shower with its intricate array of nozzles. Lucian didn't say a word to me as I looked around, just offered me a smile before he left, closing the door behind him.

I undressed and stepped inside the shower, looking at each nozzle in turn and wondering what they did. I turned the biggest one and hot water jetted out, splashing my feet and body. I gasped in surprise before I turned to the others, they had odd markings on them and I didn't know what they meant, so I decided to test them out.

The first one was pink and smaller than the rest; it filled my cupped hands with shampoo, which I lathered into my hair before rinsing. I looked for a similar nozzle that might give me conditioner and when I found it I put it in my hair, letting it sit while I looked at the other nozzles. One was soap, another held colourful and multi-scented bubbles, the last held a warm purple liquid that smelled of lilacs and lavender. I didn't know what it was but it lathered like soap so I ran it over my body.

After I smelled good and my hair was clean I turned all the nozzles tightly save for the water and I sank to the floor of the glass shower, pulling my knees to my chest, my hair hanging around my body in long, wet ropes. And then I cried. I let myself embrace the pain like I hadn't really gotten to the night before. I bawled for the life that had been taken from me, the woman who'd raised me in place of my mother. I cried for all the women John Hathorne had taken from me and then I thought of Grams again, of all the things we would miss out on together, of all the things we'd enjoyed together and of all the surreal days I would live without her.

I cried until my chest hurt and my sides ached with the force of my sobs. I cried until my eyes felt swollen and raw and my nose dripped with water and snot. I cried until I was so worn out that there were no tears left.

I stood slowly and rinsed my hair one more time before turning off the water and stepping out, while wrapping myself up in the warm and fuzzy towels. I dried off and pulled on the clothes I'd worn the day before, too tired and sad to care what I looked like, even to Lucian.

Then I went back into the living room, the smell of eggs and bacon made my mouth water and my stomach growl. Lucian sat on one of the couches, a cup of coffee in his hand. He didn't say a word as I entered just nodded to the plate of fresh food and a second cup of coffee, all made for me.

I couldn't look at him as I sat on the opposite couch, I knew he'd heard me crying in the bathroom and though I knew I had every right to mourn the loss of my grandmother I couldn't help but feel embarrassed that he'd overheard me during my worst moment of weakness. But he didn't mention the fact that I'd used up all his hot water or that I'd spent nearly an hour in the bathroom.

"I was wondering if you wanted to come with me into town." Lucian said after a long uncomfortable silence.

"Into town?" Irrational fear made my heartbeat quicken and I met his eyes.

"Vase Line," he said, his face completely blank as he watched me. "I have to meet some friends."

"For what?"

He shrugged, sipping his coffee as his emerald eyes peered at me over the rim of the cup. "I need to warn them of The Hunt. Hathorne will not stop at Genevieve; he wants to do it right this time."

I swallowed the bile that had risen at the sound of that demon's name. "What do you mean by that?"

He shrugged again. "They're Connor's words not mine. But, the only real witch the Church managed to kill was your ancestor. All of the others were innocent human women. I think he plans to kill witches and only witches."

I frowned, "They killed humans last time? But John Hathorne was head of The Hunt then too."

"What?"

I'd forgotten, I hadn't told Lucian about Hathorne being a two hundred year old freak of nature. I hadn't told him that he'd been Cadence's brother, perhaps not biologically but he'd believed he had been and I was his daughter. Because he was a sick bastard he'd found the newest in Cadence's line, the Moore witch Morgana and he'd impregnated her with me, half Moore and half whatever he was.

"In 1624 Johnathan Hathorne was recorded as the name of Cadence O'Connell's twin brother and now, two hundred and thirty years later, there is a man who fit's the name and picture of the same Johnathan Hathorne." I said, wishing I'd taken the book with me when I'd left the house yesterday and then hating myself for wishing something as inconsequential as that.

"He's two hundred and thirty years old?"

"Yes, I don't know how he did it just that somehow he made himself immortal. But I do know that he killed Cadence because she wouldn't help him become like her."

"He wanted to be Chosen?"

I nodded. "Grams and I think that Cadence was an adopted child of the Hathorne's and that they'd told Cadence and John that they were twins because they were born around the same time. Plus, Cadence was the only one in her family to have magick or her last name."

"Did they look alike?"

"Not at all but that's common with male and female fraternal twins." I said, shrugging. "John doesn't know he isn't biologically linked to Cadence or that she was

Chosen because it was her destiny. He feels she denied him something and he thought she deserved to pay, so he killed her, in the name of Christ and in front of a thousand people."

"Wow, and then two hundred and thirty years later he met Morgana?"

"Yeah, he's sick and twisted." I said, venom seeping into my voice as I thought about it. "Luckily they aren't related. But he didn't know that at the time."

Lucian blew out a long breath, shaking his head at the absurdity of the matter. "So this vendetta of his is because he wanted the magick Cadence had?"

I nodded. "He's a spoiled brat."

"Apparently," he ran a hand through his hair. "So do you want to come to town? I don't really relish the thought of leaving you alone here, where Hathorne could reach you at any time."

"Connor told me to stay here. He wouldn't lead Hathorne to us would he?"

He shrugged. "I don't know Connor all that well, I mean I did once, but that was years ago. A lot has changed since then. I know he means well and he wants to protect you and I applaud that but I think it would be best if you stay by my side at least for now. Connor won't be back for two weeks, just like he said, there's a lot to do and a lot of people to warn within that time."

I sighed, "Sure, okay."

He grinned but there was something dark in the depths of his emerald eyes. "There are clothes in the drawer in the wardrobe. You can change into some, anything you like. I have another coat in there too; I'd like you to wear it in case someone recognizes you."

"Like my coat matters."

"It's lime green love, you stick out like a sore thumb."

I smiled at that, turning to look at the bright green coat that was hung up on a hook to the right of the door. He was right, it was almost florescent. "Fine, but do you have female clothing?"

He nodded, pressing his lips together so they turned from a luscious pink to a pained white. I frowned but didn't press the matter, if Lucian had skeletons in his closet there was no reason for me to pry. He would tell me if he wanted to and if not then that was fine, it was his call.

I went into his room to change, picking out a black long sleeved shirt and a pair of snug jeans, which fit perfectly, to my surprise. Then I grabbed a knee length coat from the hanger on the door of the closet, it was surprisingly chic and I liked how I looked in it.

I went out into the living room and hung up my coat as I waited for Lucian to finish showering, having heard him close the door before the sound of running water filled the small house. I sat on the couch and looked out the window, towards Genevieve. I knew that out there was an evil man with delusions of grandeur and what was left of my beautiful Victorian house and the ashes of my beloved Grams.

I vowed I would repay him in the worst way I could, I would get revenge for the people he'd taken from me, first Mom and then Grams and two hundred and thirty years ago he'd taken my life from me, though I'd been someone else. I would repay John Hathorne for all of this and then some because evil men like him didn't deserve to win and I would make sure, if it was the last thing I did, that he lost.

Nine

VASE LINE WAS just as busy as it ever was. There were people crowding the streets either in cars or on feet and not one of them looked happy. I'd never been in Vase Line during the day and it was a completely different crowd jostling Lucian and I along the busy sidewalks on their way to work. At night it was the bar hoppers and the cheap hookers but by day it was the business men and women. It was an interesting contrast.

Lucian held my hand as we walked, pulling me back and forth to avoid people as they shouldered past us, making no attempt to avoid me. It was as if not one person in this town had ever learned manners or common courtesy. I gripped his hand as if it were a lifeline and in some respects it was, by the time we came to a winding driveway my grip had become bruising and his hand was turning red.

He pulled it free and wrapped it around my shoulders, turning me to face him as we stopped in front of his friend's driveway. "I need to tell you something."

Internal alarm bells rang inside me as my eyes narrowed almost unconsciously. "What?"

"I kind of told Bryce and Brenna that you were my fiancé."

I gaped at him, "I'm only nineteen," was all my brilliant mind could think to say to something as out of the blue as that.

"I know that."

"You're twenty one."

"I know that too."

"Why would anyone in their right mind believe we're engaged? We're too young and, oh yeah, we barely like each other. Are you insane?"

"Listen it isn't like it's my fault, I got tongue tied when Brenna asked me about you and how we met and I just told her we made our engagement official last week. It isn't a big deal, so we pretend we're together, where's the harm?"

"How am I supposed to pretend to be engaged to you? I don't know anything about you." I put my hand over my eyes, shaking my head at the absurdity of the situation. "And why wouldn't you tell them that I'm just a friend?"

"Because I couldn't okay? Just do this for me and I promise I'll help you with your vendetta against Hathorne."

"I thought you said we were coming here to warn them about The Hunt."

"We are."

"Then why did you tell them we were engaged? Why wouldn't you tell them the truth?"

He sighed, "I can't tell you now Gray, but I will, I promise. Just get through today and I'll explain everything. Please?"

I sighed and nodded, feeling sick and more than a little confused. All he'd had to say was The Hunt had started and I was the first victim. Why did he need to make it so complicated by saying something as stupid as "I'm engaged to some girl I'm bringing over"?

He took my hand and pulled me along the winding driveway to a castle-like mansion complete with stone balconies and frightening gargoyles. I didn't like it here, my stomach flip-flopped unhappily as we moved to the stone steps that led to the porch, also made of some kind of grey stone, and worsened when Lucian took the knocker in his hand and banged it against the solid oak door.

There was silence on the other side for quite some time and a large part of me hoped they weren't home and that I didn't have to continue with this stupid charade. The seconds ticked by and no one came to the door, I looked up at Lucian, his profile silhouetted against the darkening sky, his lips pressed firmly together as his eyebrows furrowed.

"Are they not here?"

"I rang before we left, they should be."

"Maybe they can't hear the knocker past all the thick stone?"

His smile was strained as his emerald eyes fastened on me, an odd emotion shining in their beautiful crystal-like depths. "Shall we use the bell then love?"

"Whatever you think is best Luke." I replied, the words feeling like bile rising from my throat.

He grinned without any inhibitions this time and pulled a long string beside the door, a gong-like sound echoed throughout the silent stone house and still no one came to answer the door.

"Let's just go, we can come back tomorrow."

"No, no. I'll check things out, you stay here."

"Yeah right," I scoffed. "You're stupid if you think that's what's going to happen. I'm the one being hunted, no way am I standing out here alone."

He rolled his eyes but didn't protest as he grabbed the knob and twisted it to the right, the door swung inward easily and the inside was black. He frowned, his beautiful eyes darting from one darkened corner to the next as he searched for his friends. An icy finger of dread ran up my back as I beheld the darkness awaiting us, I didn't want to go in there, and nothing in the world could make me.

"Luke let's go. They aren't here." I whispered, pulling on his arm.

He must have heard the fear seep into my voice because his eyes flicked to me, a frown still creasing his handsome face. "Do you feel something?"

I nodded, remembering he could read emotions. I knew that there was a power known as Sensing and that many witches carried the trait, it was a muted but effective gift. Most of the time it wasn't considered a power at all, just a sixth sense of sorts. But I'd never had it and now it was so strong it made me want to run screaming from this abandoned house.

I pressed my lips together, fighting the scream building up in the back of my throat. Something sinister was lurking in the darkness inside this house, something that I didn't want to face. I heard a scuffle much closer than I'd thought and suddenly there was a man standing in front of me.

He looked the same, I was actually a little surprised. His eyes were still so very blue and colder than ice in December. There was raw, unadulterated loathing burning in his gaze. He was still just as tall, maybe six foot, and he was built like a linebacker; he looked as formidable as the power that I could almost see crackling around him.

"Grace Moore," his voice was soft, the sound of hatred and something darker lurking in the once melodious voice I'd known in a childhood I could barely remember. "It's been a long time."

I met his gaze, trying to swallow the fear that threatened to send me screaming from him and this place. His presence was darkened by the evil he'd done and the power around him. It was almost painful to stand here, near him, when he'd hurt so many people I'd loved and watched me with victory in his eyes.

"Johnathan Hathorne." I responded my voice surprisingly strong and clear. "I've heard a lot about you."

His smile was more a bearing of teeth and just as menacing. His gaze slid to Lucian who watched him with a hatred I could never have imagined seeing on his normally happy face. There was recognition in those emerald eyes; there was something he wasn't telling me, something Hathorne had no doubt done to deserve the look he was receiving.

Hathorne didn't say anything to Lucian, his gaze slid from him to behind me and that prickle of ice cold fear walked up my spine again, making sweat bead on my forehead. This was a trap, Bryce and Brenna had never been here, for all we knew they were already dead. But no, Hathorne wanted to Hunt witches the right way, and he would want to kill them the way he'd killed Cadence all those years ago.

He smiled again and it made the chills worsen, my whole body ached with the need to run, the need to be away from him and his frightening eyes and creepy smile. "I would like to have a talk with you Grace, but this is not the place to do that."

There was a smack as a booted foot stepped onto the porch before there was a blinding pain and a disgusting cracking sound. I fell forward; right into Hathorne's waiting arms, before blackness engulfed me.

Ten

MY HEAD THROBBED in time with my heartbeat and my left cheek was pressed against a cool patch of cement. My eyelids were too heavy to open and I wondered vaguely if I was concussed. I knew there was a good chance, whoever had been behind me hadn't hit me in the right spot, I should have been out on impact, but it had taken a moment and that wasn't normal. My head ached so badly and my arms tingled painfully, as if they'd fallen asleep.

I tried to blink but my mind was still foggy and couldn't seem to send the right signals to the appropriate parts of my body.

"Grace?" the voice was familiar and yet I couldn't for the life of me match it with a face. I didn't respond or move, just tried to force my eyelids to open. "Grace."

I felt myself frown and my eyelids twitched but remain closed. I opened my mouth, the cotton taste making my tongue dry and my lips stick together. I gasped out air and suddenly there was a glass being pressed to my lips. I guzzled as much water as I could in my odd state on the floor, soaking the side of my face in the process.

"Wake up Grace."

I blinked and this time my eyes obeyed and opened. Familiar blue eyes looked back at me, a slight coldness in their depths, but they were not the same eyes I'd passed out seeing. "Connor?" I whispered, licking my still parched lips as I tried to pull myself off the floor. "Where am I?"

He helped me sit and my arms throbbed painfully. I yelped, looking up to see my arms pulled above my head by manacles and chained to the wall behind me. I frowned, my brows furrowing as I turned my gaze back to Connor.

The room was bright with ghastly yellow light. We were in some kind of basement, maybe an ancient dungeon, definitely a torture chamber of sorts. Every torture device ever recorded was down here, the Iron Maiden, several different kinds of whips, long swords and knives, something called Thumbscrews, and a whole array of iron devices I couldn't say what would do if they were used but my imagination was good enough to give me some very gory images.

I licked my dry lips nervously as my eyes fell on my brother, Connor Hathorne, a product of the cruel and sadistic Johnathan Hathorne. "Where am I Connor?" I whispered, afraid to talk too loudly in case Hathorne was here.

"He got you." Connor shook his head, something like pity shining in his cold eyes. "I told you and Lucian to stay inside, hide out, but you didn't listen."

"We were going to warn Bryce and Brenna." I said, looking up as I pulled on my chains to test their strength. Iron, too strong to break and I was weak from the hit on the head and the ice gliding through my veins. "Was I injected with something?"

Amusement glinted in his eyes for the briefest of moments. "You're sharp. It's a sedative; it'll make you drowsy and compliant for the beginning."

My throat felt as if it were closing in on itself. "The beginning?"

He shook his head, looking down at the cup in his hands. "I tried to protect you, but now there isn't anything for me to do but watch you burn."

I gulped, ignoring that for the moment. "Where's Lucian? Is he okay?"

Connor frowned. "He's at the mansion where we nabbed you. They left him after giving him a shot of the same sedative they gave you. He'll be out for a couple days unless they under-dosed him."

I blew out a breath Lucian was safe for now. Hathorne really *did* want to start The Hunt off with my family. Ending our line would end the only chance of his downfall and make it easier for him to purge the world of our people. The Moore witches were direct descendents of Cadence, the only witch he'd ever been afraid of and one of the most powerful in Wiccan history. If anyone could have stopped him it would have been one from her line.

Even in my drug hazed mind it made sense. He knew that I could get rid of him if I could explore the full extent of my powers, because not only was I Cadence's only living descendent but I was also her reincarnation and his daughter. Meaning whatever he'd done to himself to keep him young and ageless after two hundred and thirty years, flowed through my veins as well.

"Grace?" Connor looked concerned, though only slightly with his perpetual coldness seeping into those frightening blue eyes.

"My head hurts." It was true but not near what I'd been thinking. I couldn't trust Connor, no matter what he tried to say. Sure, we were siblings, but he'd lived with John his whole life, that had to have rubbed off on him at least a little.

He nodded. "Would you like a Tylenol?"

I shook my head.

"Don't be stubborn Grace. You don't need unnecessary pain, not with what Dad plans to do with you."

Disgust and fear tightened my stomach and I was afraid I'd throw up. I needed a way out of here; I needed to at least find a way to fight Hathorne off when he decided it was time to torture me. There had to be a way to tap into that explosive power of mine. But I was afraid to use it. I'd blown up three huge trees in the forest just last night and I could definitely destroy this house and everyone in it, myself included, if I wasn't careful. So the explosive power was out. But Cadence had had others and that meant that I would too, I just needed to find their triggers.

"Grace?"

I sighed and met Connor's expectant gaze, had he been asking me something? "What?"

"Do you feel dizzy?"

"No, I feel fine, except for the coldness in my veins."

"That's just the sedative, it'll wear off in about an hour." his face hardened. "After that you'll want another shot."

He made it sound so bad, so frightening, that I wanted to get out more than I wanted water at that moment. "I'm thirsty." I said softly, eyeing the yellow cup in his hand. He held it to my lips and I gulped it quickly, hoping to stave off the thirst long enough to think up a plan. I needed out, I needed to find Lucian and we needed to get as far from Genevieve and Vase Line as quickly as humanly possible.

The sound of footsteps overhead made Connor and I look up as dust fell from the wooden rafters in tiny waterfalls. Fear made my heart beat erratically and my breath quicken even as my throat closed. Connor looked at me and for the first time nothing but terror shone in his eyes. "Whatever you do don't make him mad." he whispered before he stood and took the stairs two at a time, opening the door and shutting it behind him.

I pulled at the iron manacles, the chains clanged loudly against the wall, yanking my still numb arms and making them tingle horribly. I bit back a pained yell as more dust fell from the ceiling and rumbling voices started up. I couldn't make out their words but I could tell they'd heard me and were glad I was awake.

I looked around again and I could tell why the light had been left on. They wanted me to see the tools of torture they had, the ones used back when the original Witch Hunt had burned throughout the world. They wanted me to be afraid and they wanted me to scream when they tortured me.

I wished desperately that I was with Lucian and far away from here. I wanted so bad to be back at the house, in the shower, thinking of nothing more devastating than losing my Grams. I wanted to be somewhere, anywhere, but here.

Suddenly the room around me faded, shimmering out of existence and for a moment I thought I'd passed out again. But instead I stood in the foyer of Bryce and Brenna's mansion. It wasn't as dark as it had been the last time I'd seen it and lying on the cold floor was Lucian, his eyes flitting from side to side as he dreamed. I frowned, wondering if I was dreaming and then vaguely recalling reading about a power like this, it was called astral projecting.

I shrugged before diving into Lucian's mind. There was a whirlwind of noise and colour and then I was standing beside him, gripping his hand, he was five and

I was three. It was the summer, all those years ago, and it was the last day we'd spent together.

We were standing outside with our family and friends, it was raining and we were wearing black clothes. We watched as two caskets were lowered into the ground, we didn't cry, we couldn't feel it yet. Then, the dream shifted and we were reliving the moment it happened.

Our mother's were standing in the living room talking to a man we couldn't see. They were yelling and we were afraid. The man kept saying that he wouldn't let them take Grace to Ireland, but Lucian wanted me to come, he wanted me to stay with him.

And then the dream shifted again and this time we were standing in the town square and there was the mangled and burnt bodies of two women. Grams was crying and so was another man, a man I'd never seen before but knew to be Lucian's dad.

And then we were at their graves; their headstones were brief and nondescript.

Morgana Moore
Loving Mother and Devoted Daughter
Born 1971 Died 2010
And
Lucinda McCormick
She will be missed by all who knew her.
Born 1972 Died 2010

The dream was slipping and I could feel my body being shaken somewhere far from Lucian and his sad memories. I couldn't fight the persistent shaking but I put happy memories into his mind, things I'd remembered from that year, playing pirates and making mud pies. I kissed the little version of Lucian before I was pulled back into my own body and my own bitter memories.

Eleven

THE SMILE I received upon waking was more like a predator sizing up its prey. There was no misunderstanding Hathorne's intent as he looked at me, his eyes blazing with white hot hate, his smile slow and menacing. He planned to hurt me, to humiliate me, and he planned to do it with the arsenal of torture he'd put together during his two hundred and thirty years of extended life.

He sat back on his feet, resting his elbows on his thighs as he met my gaze. "So, it's true."

I just looked at him.

"You're her reincarnation." he clarified. "You look just like her you know. It's been quite some time since I've seen you little one."

"You're sick." I spat the word as if it were a curse. "Cadence was your sister and you procreated with someone from her line."

He grinned, "Cadence O'Connell was not my sister, and you know that."

I didn't respond, my eyes narrowed.

"She was adopted, we both knew it, but it wasn't something you talked about, not back then. She was my sister for all intents and purposes but biologically she was nothing to me and when I met Morgana I didn't feel sickened at the thought of being with her. Actually, I felt the first shreds of happiness."

His smile was wistful and it almost caught me of guard. *Almost.* It only took a moment for the hate that burned behind his cold blue eyes to return and he was Hathorne again, not my father.

"Where did you go when you were sleeping?" He asked.

"I dreamt, it's what people do."

His smile was vicious. "You astral projected. Where did you go? To see your boyfriend and his friends? To warn them?"

"I don't know what you're talking about."

"Don't lie to me Grace."

"Just because we share blood doesn't mean you can talk to me like I'm your daughter. You abandoned me after you killed my mom, don't sit there and act as if I owe you something."

His hand shot out so fast that I didn't realize what had happened until pain exploded across my face, black spots danced across my vision as blood dribbled out of my nose. I gasped, blinking past the blackness as I moved my head to meet his gaze. That same unadulterated hatred was looking back at me.

"Don't you dare talk back to me." he spat, his voice so thick with anger I could barely understand his words. "You are incredibly stupid. You're chained to a wall with an array of torture devices sitting around you and you dare to snap at me?"

I spat at him, blood covered his face along with a trickle of spittle. Underneath my blood his face reddened and he snapped his fingers, standing. He kicked out and his foot hit me in the ribs, sending me against the wall as pain coursed up my left side.

"Unchain her." He snarled his voice so demonic it frightened me.

Men came forward, unchained me and replaced my iron manacles with their meaty fists. I was pulled forward, scrapping my knees along the cement floor as they dragged me into the middle of the room. Hathorne moved to stand behind me. The sound of iron scraping across metal made goose bumps skitter across my arms.

"You're a little brat," He was saying, picking things up and putting them down as he considered how to start my torture. "You don't know what you're talking about; you have no idea what I'm capable of."

My mouth went dry as the crack of a whip echoed around me. He'd chosen his first weapon; he was going to degrade me by whipping me. An ancient memory surfaced then, he'd done this to me before, in another place and another time. I bit my lip to keep from whimpering.

"I'll show you why you should listen to me, why you should obey me." The whip cracked again and this time it licked at my skin, my back arched against the pain as I swallowed my scream. I wouldn't give him the satisfaction of making me scream. But tears poured from my eyes, dripping onto the concrete as he lashed my back, over and over again.

It wasn't long, maybe five minutes, but it felt like an eternity. I was thrown forward, my head slamming against the cement with a sickening slapping sound. Blackness picked at my vision as tears made everything blur. Hathorne moved to my head and squatted, his voice low as he spoke. "Don't disrespect me again little one."

When he was gone I fell into pain-filled dreams.

John had pretended he'd loved me, he'd pretended he cared that I was locked up like a dog. But today I realized it was all a lie. Because today I learned that it was Mother who'd sent me to this place, because the Goddess had given me magick and not her.

John was sent into the dungeon and I smiled at him, I hadn't been allowed to see any of my family while I waited for my trial and I was overjoyed to see him standing there. But he was somber, his eyes cold and distant.

"Are you here to take me home?" I asked.

He just looked at me, pity shining in his eyes. "I'm here to tell you that there isn't anything we can do. You won't have a trial, you will burn at sunset."

My mouth went dry as I frowned. "But I'm a Hathorne, how can they not give me a trial?"

"You are not a Hathorne Cade, you never were."

When he left I cried until I was so exhausted I dropped into fitful sleep. My family would let me burn, people I'd always loved and had always assumed loved me back were going to watch me die because they were jealous over something I'd had no choice over. How completely unfair and unjust our world was becoming that I almost laughed at the absurdity of it all.

Almost.

Twelve

WHEN I WOKE up for the third time Connor was there, lying strips of cloth onto the bloody lashes crisscrossing my back. I didn't know what he was using to clean them but it stung so badly it made tears spill down my cheeks and pool on the cement floor.

"Are you awake?"

I grunted, in too much pain to carry on any semblance of a normal conversation. The liquid he was dipping the cloths into was yellow and smelly. I winced every time he touched me, sending pain shooting throughout my entire body.

"Stop jumping Grace, you're just making it worse."

"Shut up," I snapped. "Go away."

Connor's hands stopped for a moment as I felt his eyes on my face. "What?"

"I said go away."

"Why?"

"Because, you're at fault here too. You could have helped me, you could have stopped them and you wouldn't. I don't need your sympathy or your help; it hasn't done me any good so far."

Connor exhaled but didn't move; he dipped another bit of cloth into the cold, yellow liquid and then gently smoothed it across my aching back. He didn't say another word as he helped me sit up and pull on a new shirt.

I was in so much pain and lashing out at Connor was the last thing I wanted to do but I'd raised a few good points. This whole time he'd been trying to protect me including when he had sent Lucian to us with the message. But nothing had helped, not advanced warning, not a safe haven. It was as if Hathorne knew my moves before I made them.

I mentally kicked myself for being so naïve. I'd trusted Connor because it had seemed like blood would triumph over evil, but that evil ran in his veins as much as it did in mine and I'd been stupid to trust a product of Johnathan Hathorne.

Connor helped me to my feet before leading me back to the wall and clasping the chains to my wrists. He didn't say anything to me but his eyes told me that he was done trying to help. He moved away from me and up the stairs before I had a chance to say anything, not that I would have if I'd wanted to.

I leaned back against the cold cement wall and looked over at the torture tools Hathorne kept around me. The whip was still dripping with blood and mocked me from its holder. I fought to keep the nausea and tears at bay but it was no use, I sobbed, quietly, because I knew there was no way I could get out. Hathorne had me chained in iron manacles and kept injecting me with some kind of sedative that dulled my powers to almost nonexistence. I couldn't fight him or his acolytes. I couldn't move from this spot even to look for a window. I was trapped and the only way I would get out is if I could get someone to break me out.

Clomping footsteps overhead made me look up at the ceiling. The rumble of angry voices echoed down to me but I couldn't make out their words. I heard Connor move into the room, his voice mingling with the others. They quieted and Connor asked a muffled question.

I couldn't hear what Hathorne said to his son but I could hear the hurried and angry words and my already cold blood became a hard lump of ice. I didn't know where Hathorne went when he wasn't here but I knew it always had something to do with The Hunt. I would be the first witch to die, he'd make sure of it, but that might be sooner than I expected.

I looked over at the tools of agony again and sighed in relief. I wouldn't be tortured into submission by my own father. I'd be killed and then it would all begin. I let out a breath as my resolve began to waver. I couldn't just die; my death would bring an apocalypse of sorts to all witches. He'd purge the world like he hadn't been able to during the last Hunt. If I died he'd continue The Hunt until not one witch was left standing, I couldn't let that happen.

I sighed and closed my eyes. I didn't know how to trigger my astral projection power but I would try anyway. I needed back up and the only way to get it would be to send my astral self to Lucian who was probably already awake. I pictured him in my minds eye: his unruly black hair and his amazing emerald eyes, his muscular, six foot body and that devil-may care smile that always seemed to be lurking beneath his other expressions.

I opened my eyes only to find myself no longer sitting in Hathorne's dank dungeon but standing in front of Lucian's small house in the forest between Genevieve and Vase Line. He was standing outside surrounded by a cluster of people, talking softly about something I couldn't hear.

I cleared my throat and everyone jumped, looking over at me with wide, fearful eyes. All save for Lucian, a pain like I'd never seen before shone out of those perfect emerald eyes and I knew what he was thinking.

"I'm not dead."

A slight smile pulled at the side of his lips. "Then what are you?"

"I'm astral projecting. Apparently its one of my many powers." The people around him started to murmur in shocked, frightened voices but I ignored them. "I've been taken by Hathorne and I think I'm somewhere in Genevieve."

"Why Genevieve?"

"Because it only makes sense that he would want to burn me there. Cadence was the last, and only, witch killed during the trials and she was burned in the town square. I'm her reincarnation and the beginning of The Hunt, so he'll burn me in Genevieve."

"I can be there by tomorrow."

"Good. Try not to take too long, I have a feeling he's going to burn me tomorrow, around sunset."

Lucian frowned, fear seeping into his expression. "Why would you think that?"

I smiled even as my astral form began to fade. "Don't be silly Luke, he never intended to keep me for days and torture me, he wants to start The Hunt and if you're late he will."

With that I returned to the dungeon and my pained body, closing my eyes against the pain and fear that licked at my insides and made my mind scream in fear. If Lucian didn't get to Genevieve by tomorrow I would be dead, burned in front of a town that had branded me a witch since the day I was born and The Hunt would truly begin.

Thirteen

I DIDN'T KNOW how long I was chained to the dungeon wall below Hathorne's lair; it could have been one day or several. The sedative had burned out of my system and I woke alert and in control for the first time in what felt like forever. This time, when my eyes opened, no one sat in front of me, mocking me and I didn't see those familiar blue eyes that haunted my nightmares when they didn't haunt my waking hours.

I couldn't hear anything from the room above and that frightened me, though I couldn't have said why. Most people would assume he'd left, that he'd gone wherever he went during the day, but I knew better. It was too quiet and that never bodes well, not for anyone.

I looked up, there were two iron squares drilled into the cement above me and welded onto them were thick metal loops where my chains glided noisily, giving me some room to move, but not enough to ease the ache in my shoulders or the sharp pain from my whip marks. The loops were welded poorly and made of something weaker than iron, if I pulled hard enough I could probably rip my chains from the wall, but I wouldn't get far. Hathorne and his cronies would be down here as soon as they heard me break free of the cement.

But I was afraid, I could feel my death approaching, I knew he'd picked today as my death day and the beginning of his vendetta against all witches. I knew that I would burn today if Lucian didn't make it and I was afraid to sit here and wait for rescue. I was a Moore, I could fight my way out if I had to, and I did have to, because I would not die today.

I leaned forward to test the length of the chains, I could move several inches forward but that was it, enough room to lean on my knees and pull with all my strength. So that's what I did, I pushed myself to my knees and leaned forward, practically letting the metal hold all of my weight, keeping me from falling face first onto the cement floor.

I pulled, grunting with the effort, but the loops didn't budge. I sighed, twisting my hands in the chains and yanking as hard as I could. Still, the loops stayed strong.

I turned the best I could, practically wrapping myself up in the chains, and I put my feet on the cement wall, pushing with all my strength. There was a groan of metal but it didn't pull free. I yanked again, pulling with my hands even as I pushed with my feet. Another groan, louder this time. I stopped, resting with my feet on the wall and my body in the air as I held myself off the floor with the metal chains. I listened for Hathorne and his men, wondering if they'd heard the metal groan and would come to investigate.

But there was still no sound from above.

I exhaled and yanked again, pulling and pushing as hard as I could, tendons straining against my skin. The groan was so loud this time that I knew if anyone was upstairs they'd heard me. But I didn't stop, just continued pushing and pulling until the loops broke free of the iron squares and I fell to the floor in a heap.

"Oaf," I huffed but grinned to myself, standing slowly so I wouldn't jostle my wounds. The chains clanged to the floor, and I hoped I could use them as a weapon and not brain myself in the process. I edged towards the stairs, looking up at the small wooden door and wondering if I could make it out without getting caught.

I crept up the stairs after I wrapped the chains around my forearms. When I came to the door I pressed my ear against it, listening for any sounds that could alert me to the presence of Hathorne, Connor or the acolytes. But again there was only silence. Fear and something sinister crept up my spine as I twisted the knob and slowly pushed the door open.

My senses kicked in to overdrive as I scanned the kitchen in front of me, it looked normal, especially for Genevieve. There were normal things, like a fridge and stove but also papers and garbage littering the floor and countertops. No one was in here; no one was guarding my door.

But there was that familiar tingling creeping up my spine while alarm bells rang loudly from within. It felt like the mansion had, cold and abandoned, exactly what they wanted me to think it was, but my senses knew better.

I pulled the chains down so they could be swung as weapons but not so low that they dragged loudly on the floor. I moved quietly through the kitchen, my eyes roving over everything I passed and every darkened corner where an enemy could be lurking. I moved into a hallway with too many doors and the hair on the back of my neck stood on end. I gripped the chains until they bit into my hands.

I moved slowly, turning to look behind me even as my eyes turned to watch my front. Someone was still here, and if it was Hathorne that meant his men were lying in wait somewhere, probably to sedate me and return me to my stone prison. I wouldn't go back down there, not for anything.

A man stepped out of the shadows and I didn't think, just acted. I swung my chains, hitting him in the face and chest and sending him flailing to the ground, out cold. Another man stepped forward and I recognized him as one of the men who'd held me while Hathorne whipped me, so I didn't think twice about whipping him with my irons chains.

Every man who stepped out of the shadows was welcomed with an iron chain whipping across their faces, I was enraged and bloodthirsty and I whipped and hit everyone in my path, moving towards the door and my freedom.

When the last man fell to the floor, bloody and unconscious, I ran for it. I didn't get far though because my limbs wouldn't obey my brain as they suddenly stopped cold, freezing me inches from the door. The sound of clapping, from somewhere behind me, grating on the last of my nerve.

"Well done," his voice was worse than any kind of venom and just as frightening. "Turn around."

My limbs obeyed, turning me to face him. "What have you done to me?" My voice was awkward and stilted.

He smiled and cocked a brow, not responding and not denying that he was the one controlling my body. "Come to me."

Jerkily my legs wobbled over to where he stood in the shadows, only his ice cold eyes were visible. Anger burned through me but I couldn't take control of my own body. I stood in front of him, looking into those frightening eyes. I didn't want to be here, I'd rather fight and escape and run from him. But my body wouldn't obey my mind and it was the worse kind of torture.

"You will give me your magick willingly." His voice was almost a croon but the coldness in his eyes were at odds with the sound. "You kept them from me for two hundred and thirty years but today you will hand them over, *willingly.*"

I knew what he was doing, what he wanted from me, and my mind begged me to keep quiet. But I wasn't in control anymore and there was no inhibitions, nothing to keep me from saying the words that would remove my magick and hand them over to Judge Johnathan Hathorne.

My mouth opened despite the screaming voice in my mind. He'd let me think I could control a part of myself, lulling me into a false sense of security, but I'd been naïve to think he couldn't control my voice too.

"Say it Grace, give me your magick."

Tears blurred my vision as my mouth opened again. "I give you my magick."

A whistling wind engulfed us, stealing away my breath and magick and handing them over to my worst nightmare, my own father. I gasped for air even as I begged for my magick back, but it was too late, I'd said the words and now I was empty, hollow, without any magick to prove I'd been Chosen by the Goddess.

I fell to my knees as his hold on me vanished with the wind. He looked down at me; the coldness in his eyes was underlined by triumph. I sobbed despite myself and he kicked me, hard, in the side, sending me sprawling to the floor where the back of my head hit the corner of the table with a sickening crunching noise. I fell into oblivion, hoping that I was finally dead and that it was all over.

Fourteen

I WAS SO hot. Sweat soaked my body, making my bloody clothes stick to me. Tears blurred my vision and heat like I've never known before stifled my breath and made me feel as if I were being smothered.

I opened my eyes, blinking away tears, I knew where I was. In my town they had kept Cadence's pyre in perfect condition, as a warning to the witches they thought lived among them. And now, because of their hatred, I was burning.

I saw all of the people I had grown up with, people who had branded me a witch from the time I was born. They watched with looks of surprised horror on their faces but not one of them would stand up for me, not one of them would help *the witch*.

I could hear Hathorne's deep voice, ranting on and on about Satan and evil and the bible. "Thou shalt not suffer a witch to live." He boomed, his cold eyes meeting mine for a brief moment, victory shining in their blue depths. "And is it wrong for us to follow the tenants of our beloved Book?"

No one said anything. How could they dispute the teachings of the Church?

"Like her family, Grace Moore is a witch, and she will burn this night."

In this life there were no cheers or jeering. There was a frightening silence I had never known before. And it was heavy with fear and worry. God-fearing people had learned a long time ago that burning women was wrong and that men like the one before them were the real demons in disguise.

But no one would argue with him, and no one would stand up for me.

I watched as the fire grew. It was so hot and I gulped in air. I was afraid and sweating, the heat making my eyes water and my heart beat too quickly. I couldn't die, I had to save the others.

But the fire was making it hard to think and I could no longer see the townspeople through the tears that welled in my eyes. The heat intensified and licked at my left leg. I screamed in agony and the fire quickened, burning a whole through my jeans and running up the length of my leg.

I could feel the skin melting away, sizzling and popping with a pain I'd never known before. I screamed again, my head thrown back, my eyes on the starry sky above. I begged the Goddess to help me, I screamed as the pain in my leg moved up to my thigh, the fire eating away at it.

But no one came, the Goddess didn't smite my enemy and the fire was moving up faster and faster as time passed. The smell alone was putrid.

Suddenly, there was a loud popping noise that dulled the sound of the roaring fire for a moment. Familiar green eyes looked at me from behind the wall of fire and I thought of Lucian. I missed him, his quick smile and beautiful eyes. I remembered how he'd looked after we kissed and I wished he was here, even just to say goodbye.

I closed my eyes, trying to ignore the pain as I remembered the man who'd helped me, who'd saved my life and told me of The Hunt. I remembered the child I'd spent a year of my life playing with, the boy who'd loved me and made me laugh.

I cried for him, screaming out his name. but I was beyond hoping for help now. And then, with a whispered word I barely heard, the fire was snuffed out, sending choking smoke billowing around me. The pain was too much now and my mind was going, falling into oblivion.

Strong arms came around me and I thought of Lucian again. I sighed happily, the pain numbed as my mind blackened. "Love Lucian," I whispered, feeling the arms tightened around me. And then I fell into oblivion, hoping for death.

*   *   *

I stood on the platform, my arms tied behind me and my body tied around the stake that would play as my pyre. Everyone looked up at me, hatred burning in their gazes but I ignored it, I looked to the heavens and prayed.

When I opened my eyes again the most glorious couple stood before me. My eyes fell on the man first, his whole being seemed to scream wild. His hair was the colour of sunshine and fell to his shoulders in perfect waves. Protruding from the glowing, ever-moving hair, were two beautiful antlers, made of perfect white bone. His face was just as beautiful as every other part of him; his eyes were completely white but seemed to glow with their own inner light. His body was hard packed with sinewy muscles and the only clothes he wore was a loin cloth that ended in a point to his knees and a pair of furry boots.

Beside him the woman was just as glorious and impossible. Her hair was the most amazing brown and wind blown, falling to her waist in long ropes and intertwined with twigs and flowers. On her head was a perfect wreath of oak and roses. Her eyes were the same strange white and her lips were luscious and soft-looking. Her body was as sinewy and muscular as the man's beside her but it was still curvy and feminine. She was trim and yet vivacious, her body covered in the same material the man's loin cloth was made of but it fell to her ankles and dipped low around her breasts. Her feet were clad in the same furry boots.

She smiled at me, her voice seemed to invade my mind but I welcomed it because it brought with it that loving white light. **You have done well**. *She whispered, smiling.* **You will join me in the Summerlands**.

I wanted to ask about my baby, Althea, I wanted to know if she was going to live and carry on my line, I wanted to know if she would be safe. But I couldn't say any of these things; I couldn't even open my mouth.

Your line will be strong Cadence; I have plans for your children. *And with that she touched my cheek and took away the pain of the fire, taking me with her to the Summerlands and my new home...*

I gasped myself awake, trying to move away from the dream despite the warming light that had made me feel safe and comforted. I kicked but couldn't seem to make myself move, I was wrapped in something heavy and my eyes felt droopy and gritty.

"Gray," his voice floated to me on a wave of sweetness and I turned to see familiar emerald eyes.

I smiled, "Am I dead?"

Those eyes narrowed, "Of course not."

"But the fire, I remember the pain so vividly."

"It was a close call." His voice was reluctant as if it hurt him to admit it.

"Am I hurt?"

Silence greeted my words and I frowned, searching his face for an answer, but he'd put up that mask, disconnecting himself from the situation. "Yes," he whispered. "Does it hurt?"

"Does what hurt?" Fear made my voice crack at the end and I swallowed, hating the weakness.

He sat up and pulled the heavy covers off my body. I was lying in a thin white cotton nightgown because my leg was mutilated. Up to my thigh, just above my knee, my skin was puckered and burned, leaving only red and sizzled flesh. I choked on my sob even as a whimper escaped my lips.

I'd never been vain but this was horrible, the skin was grotesque and pulled too tightly in some places while hanging off others. The flesh was red and black and cracked in places. It looked deforming and gross but I couldn't feel the pain that I knew had to accompany it.

"Pain?" I croaked, blinking hard to keep from crying. I was alive; I was safe with Lucian, that's what I needed to remember now. I couldn't fall to pieces over something like this.

"We gave you something for it."

Great, more drugs. I nodded; too petrified by the sight of my leg to really care that they'd given me something to keep me from feeling unnecessary pain. I almost wished

I didn't need to think now, that pain was clouding my vision, so I didn't have to see what had become of my leg.

"The others?" I whispered, closing my eyes against the sight, though it was branded on the inside of my eyelids.

"Safe," he put his hand underneath my chin, moving my face so that I had to meet his eyes. "Are you okay?"

I started to shake my head but stopped myself. Sure I'd been whipped and hit and almost killed the same way I had in a past life and sure my leg was mutilated and I was drugged so much I was surprised I could think. But I was alive, I was safe and for now The Hunt was postponed until Hathorne could bring me back and finish the job he'd started with my leg.

"I'm fine." I said but it came out sounding as bad as I knew it was going to be. A lie.

"You don't need to be Gray; you've been through a lot."

I nodded, unconvinced. I wasn't supposed to feel sorry for myself and wallow. I was supposed to protect the other witches from Hathorne and a big part of that was keeping myself alive.

Lucian sighed and I met his eyes, seeing an odd tenderness in their depths. "Let's talk about something else shall we? Just for a moment let's pretend we're normal and have a conversation. How does that sound?"

I grinned. "More than wonderful."

He smiled. "You said something before you fell asleep," his gaze drop from mine as a blush crept up his cheek and I wondered what I'd said. "Do you remember?"

I shook my head, "Tell me."

He came closer, his minty breath brushing my face as his hand came up to touch my cheek, ever so gently.

"You said "love Lucian"." he grinned as a blush reddened my cheeks now.

"I did not."

Hurt shot across his face for an instant and then was replaced with his usual care-free grin. He shrugged. "Don't believe me, but I heard you."

I smiled and met his eyes, my gaze flicking between his perfect emerald ones. "I do love you Lucian. I realized it when I was burning and the idea of never seeing you hurt me to my core. I remember the fun we'd had as kids, not just the fighting. I liked you back then and I like you now."

His grin was so sweet that it made my heart skitter happily. "And I've always loved you Gray. Since that summer I spent with you."

We kissed then, passionately but also lovingly. It was the sweetest most romantic kiss I'd ever experienced and was belied by our fear of losing the other. I clung to him, trying to forget about my leg and The Hunt, but I knew I couldn't give in to something so pleasing while such evil things were happening, things only I could end.

I pulled back and ran my finger tips over his stubbled chin. It looked as if he hadn't shaved in days and dark circles underlined his eyes as if he hadn't had a good night sleep since I'd been taken. "Are you okay?" I asked, worry filling my body.

"You're safe," he replied with a shrug, as if that answered my question.

I smiled and shook my head. "There's something I need to tell you."

He frowned, his eyes darkening. "Go ahead."

"Johnathan Hathorne took my magick from me."

Lucian frowned again, his gaze flitting back and forth between my eyes. "What do you mean he took it? You have to give it willingly."

I shrugged. "He took control of my body and forced me to say the words. I want to end this, but I need my magick back."

Lucian ran a hand over his hair, "There's a ritual we can do but it's dangerous, you could die."

"If I don't do it many more people are going to die. Besides, I'm vulnerable without my magick."

He nodded, reluctance shining in his eyes. "I'll go speak to Brenna, rest for now, let the painkillers burn out of your system and we'll do it later tonight."

He kissed me quickly, pain shining in his eyes. I knew he didn't like the idea of doing a ritual that could kill me but there was more at stake than my life, and he knew it as well as I did.

I closed my eyes when the door snapped shut behind him. I tried to sleep but blissful oblivion wouldn't come to my rescue this time. There was so much occupying my mind and though it was completely selfish the main thing was my leg. It didn't hurt but it was beyond repair now and mangled to the point that it was unrecognizable. I felt bad for caring more about my leg than getting my magick back, but I tried to stifle both feelings as I closed my eyes against tears and gut wrenching sobs.

It wasn't long before the pain came for me, sending me into a fevered sleep.

Fifteen

WHEN I WOKE Lucian carried me out of the room and into the cool night, gently setting me down in the center of a loose circle made up of the witches he'd warned about The Hunt. Brenna and Bryce were there, I knew, but I had yet to meet them and was only vaguely aware of my surroundings, the pain was so blinding I was surprised I wasn't screaming.

Lucian moved away from me, standing with the others in the circle but moving as close as he could despite an angry rebuke from someone I couldn't see. A beautiful woman with flaming red hair and dark, almost black, eyes moved into the circle, she wore a black cloak overtop of a gown made of green silk. In one hand she held an old book made of red leather and in the other a ceremonial dagger, an athame, we called it.

She started to chant in a language I didn't know, the words were guttural and thick, making it sound like she was growling more than saying anything. Wind whistled through the trees, similar to the wind that had taken my magick from me and the woman's voice rose as the sound of the wind increased.

She bent after a few more grunts were uttered and met my gaze. "I'm going to cut you, do you consent?"

I nodded and she frowned. "You have to consent."

"Yes, you may take my blood." I whispered.

She cut my wrist, slitting my skin almost to my elbow. I barely felt the pain as heat scorched through me and the wind whipped around us. I screamed for Lucian as a burning like I'd never known ran through my veins, bringing with it the magick I'd lost. With the heat came a warm white light as the Goddess' magick came to me, warming me and filling me like I'd never felt it before. I wondered vaguely what the heat had been for.

I screamed again and thudding sounded around me as everyone in the circle was thrown onto their backs. The wind died and my arm was covered with a dark shirt. My head felt light and my vision was blurry as I blinked up at Lucian. He shone in the moonlight where it touched his skin; he'd taken off his shirt and pressed it to my bloody and dripping arm.

Groans and murmurs met my ears as everyone climbed to their feet, moving to surround us. I didn't recognize a single face save for Lucian's and I frowned up at them even as the loss of blood started to make my brain fuzzy and my eyes droop.

"She need's stitches." Lucian snapped at a man with the same bright red hair the woman who'd performed the ceremony. "Hurry up, get the kit."

The man ran into the house and came back with a white emergency kit, setting it down beside Lucian and whispering in his ear. Lucian frowned at him but started opening the kit, muttering something I couldn't catch. He pulled out a huge needle and medical thread and I passed out before he'd even begun.

*   *   *

When I woke again there was no pain, though the morphine had burned out of my system during the ritual. My arm throbbed, but dully, and itched like mad. I tried to sit up but strong hands pushed me down. An instinct I hadn't known I had kicked into overdrive and I kicked and flailed, trying to throw my enemy off of me. I wouldn't be held down and I wouldn't be constrained, not again. I was tired of being beaten and whipped and fettered. I would fight even if it killed me.

"Gray!" Lucian screamed and I stopped flailing for a moment to blink up at the person holding me down. "Hold still," he panted. "I'm not going to hurt you."

I did as he asked but reluctance and fear burned through me, apparently I'd developed a new phobia. "You need to get up slowly. You're injured, remember?"

I nodded as he moved his hands off of me and sat on the side of my bed. I sat slowly, being careful not to jostle the wounds I couldn't feel. "What happened to me? Why can't I feel any pain?"

Lucian frowned and something dark flitted across his face. "The Goddess' magick helped heal some of your wounds, though they'll all scar."

"Which ones were healed?"

He looked at me, "You can walk on your leg now, I'm sure of it, but it doesn't look any better. It's not red now, just white and scarred. Your whip marks are still there but they're faint white scars now. However, since I had to stitch you up after the ceremony your arm still needs to heal."

I don't know if it was morbid fascination or masochism but I suddenly needed to see my leg, to see what he was talking about. I told him this and he blew out a put-upon sigh and helped me with the blankets, being excruciatingly gentle to a leg that no longer pained me.

He unwrapped it and then moved aside to allow me to inspect it. It looked better than it had the day before, if I had truly been asleep for a night, but it still wasn't pretty. The skin was white and puckered and stretched too taut in some places while hanging slightly in others, just like before. It was deforming, just like I'd assumed from the beginning, but it wasn't red and inflamed and that gave me some measure of comfort. Though, not much.

I bit back the whimper that was building in my throat as I turned my head away from the sight, tears blurring my vision. Lucian rewrapped my leg and moved to sit in the chair beside my bed; I wondered how long he'd been sleeping there.

"There's bad news Gray." Lucian said after a long moment of silence as I fought to regain control.

"Bad news?" I asked, surprised when my voice didn't crack. "What do you mean?"

I turned to look at him but he was looking at his hands, strong and round, instead of at me. "Hathorne spent two days looking for you, he sent out a number of his men, but no one could find you." He smiled slightly at that and I wanted to ask what he meant but held my tongue. His smile faded. "He's decided The Hunt must go on, even if you aren't the first to die."

Silence descended as I absorbed the meaning behind his words. "He killed someone?"

Lucian let out a breath, running a hand through his hair as he tried to look at me, but he couldn't seem to meet my gaze. "Yesterday, while you were sleeping, Brenna and I slipped into Genevieve to see what was happening and how far Hathorne was in his search of you. When we got there, a woman was being burned on the same stake he'd tried to burn you on."

I gasped for air, feeling as if someone had sucker punched me in the gut. "How do you know she was a witch?"

"I told you, he's doing it right this time."

I didn't know if 'right' was the word to use but I let it go. I'd hoped I could protect the others by escaping Hathorne's prison and then being rescued before I burned, but I'd been wrong. He'd been planning this for two hundred and thirty years, there was no way that he was going to let something as insignificant as my life stop him from completing his goal. I felt sick at the thought of that witch's death, she hadn't been warned, she'd had no idea that Hathorne was alive or that she was in danger.

"So it's begun," I whispered, meeting his gaze. "We have to warn the others."

He nodded, "There are a lot, I don't know if we'll be able to find all of them before he burns them."

"We're going to have to try. You know some, I assume?"

He nodded, his lips pushed together tightly.

"And Brenna and Bryce?"

"They know more than I do." he said with a nod.

"Well, that's a start, the other's we'll have to search for. I'm not going to let him win."

Lucian nodded, "We'll search for them love. I promise. But for now, you need some rest."

"I've been sleeping for days, I want to get up."

He sighed and moved to my side, helping me out of my tangled blankets and onto the cold wooden floor. I was surprised how sturdy I was on my burned leg. He kept one hand on the small of my back, preparing to catch me if I fell, but I didn't and we made it to the living room.

The woman with bright red hair who'd performed the ceremony sat beside the man with the red hair, heads bent towards one another as they whispered. When they saw us they straightened and their dark eyes narrowed.

"Lucian she isn't to be out of bed." Her accent was Irish and thicker than Lucian's. Her eyes fell on me. "How do you feel?"

There wasn't anything in her expression that told me she truly cared so I shrugged, turning to look at Lucian. He smiled at me, but it didn't reach his eyes. "Gray, this is Brenna and Bryce."

I turned back to them, surprised that these were his so called friends. They were twins that much I could tell and they seemed unhappy and less than friendly. "Nice to meet you."

Bryce harrumphed, crossing his arms. "There is nothing nice about any of this." He muttered, his dark eyes glaring up at me.

Anger boiled my blood. "No one knows that better than me," I snapped. "And you know what? I never asked for any of this, so calm down and tell me why the hell you two look so pissed off."

Their eyes went wide with surprise; only Lucian seemed amused. Brenna motioned to the door, "See for yourself."

Lucian frowned as I wobbled over, throwing open the door and gasping as I took in the sight. Around twenty witches were sitting or standing in the clearing, little kids were splashing in the stream despite the cold, and all of them turned to look at us when they heard the door creak open.

"Bloody hell," Lucian mutter, his breath tickling my ear.

I nodded my agreement as the crowd burst into applause and cheers. I frowned at them, what the hell were they cheering about? We were being hunted by a mad man and I was living proof that he was more than psychotic. "Hey!" I yelled over the cheering. "What the hell are you doing here?"

A very pregnant woman stepped forward, holding the hand of a five year old boy. She smiled at us, her face lighting up as she met my gaze. "We heard about The Hunt and the sacrifices you've made. We're here to help, in any way we can."

Lucian cursed behind me again, this time loud enough to be heard.

"You shouldn't be here, you should have ran as far and as fast as you could. Hathorne wants us dead in the worst possible way, *we* aren't going to battle him, I am going to end it and every other witch is going to hide until its safe."

The woman smiled as if I were the silliest girl she'd ever met. "This is our battle too and we will stand by you."

I opened my mouth to argue but I could see in each face that they were resolute in their decision to fight Hathorne. He was threatening them as much as me, they had every right to fight if they wanted to, but there was no way in hell the woman in front of me was fighting. I'd lock her up if I had to.

I turned to Lucian who smiled at me with that same tenderness that made my insides quiver. "We're really doing this?" I whispered.

He grinned and looked over my head. "It doesn't look like we have a choice."

I sighed, turning back. "Then let The Hunt begin."